THE EXALTED
AND THE ABASED

Damian Murphy is the author of *Daughters of Apostasy* (Snuggly Books, 2017), *The Star of Gnosia* (Snuggly Books, 2018), *The Acephalic Imperial* (snuggly Books, 2020), and *The Narcissus Variations* (Mount Abraxas Press, 2021), among other collections and novellas. He was born and lives in Seattle, Washington.

I0591447

DAMIAN MURPHY

THE EXALTED
AND THE ABASED

THIS IS A SNUGGLY BOOK

ISBN: 978-1-64525-082-1

Contents

THE EXALTED AND THE ABASED

We are nothing; what we search for is everything.
—Friedrich Hölderlin

The Ivory Sovereign

ALBIN clasped his cigarette between two fingers as if it were the only thing that justified his presence in the world. He stood in the shelter of a covered doorway while the increasing downpour brought fresh color to the cobblestones. His attention was fixed on one of the buildings that stood on the opposite side of the deserted city square. Three tall, arched windows dominated the upper stories of the edifice, their surfaces made opaque by the reflection of the setting sun. His attention was particularly drawn to a panel of white stone in the center of the painted brick façade.

The panel featured a carving of an undecorated throne that was slightly angled to one side. Its emptiness suggested a deficiency that resonated with Albin's own internal state. A title—*The House of the Ivory Sovereign*—was spelled out in finely-wrought letters across the top of the panel. He placed the cigarette between his lips as he contemplated the display. Where then, he wondered, is the sovereign to be found?

Beneath the leftmost of the two wide archways that spanned the lower section of the building could be seen a row of leather carriages. These were alternately red and black and were each just large enough for two passengers to fit inside. They were attached to a rail that ran along the wooden floor and which continued beneath the rightmost arch into the depths of the house. A ticket booth stood between the two arches just beneath the empty throne. The booth was occupied by an older gentleman in a suit that looked as if it was a little too small for him. His hands lay gently folded on the surface of the counter and his gaze was trained to one side. He seemed to avoid looking directly at Albin. His impeccable dress, along with his thin, white hair and trim mustache, gave him the appearance of a retired civil servant.

As incongruous as the façade was, with its enigmatic title, it was so perfectly integrated with the surrounding architecture that the unsuspecting eye might pass right over it. One could almost mistake it for a quaint hotel, were it not for the ticket booth and carriages. Albin had immediately recognized the institution. It was nothing less than a *mystery house*—a sort of carnival attraction sometimes found on quiet city streets, inconspicuously placed among less colorful enterprises. He'd frequented a number of them in his younger days, often taking a long bus ride in order to visit one in a neighboring city. He was surprised that such a thing could still be found in a provincial town like this one. He'd assumed that they were entirely a thing of the past.

Albin had been taking somewhat of a sabbatical. A catastrophic series of events had erupted into his life and had not ceased their destructive arc until they'd laid waste to the fruits of half a lifetime of careful planning. Before the cataclysm could be stopped, he'd lost not only his career, but his marriage and his dignity as well. By the time he'd become aware of the extent of the problem, the specter had moved on and the damage was irreversible.

A ruined man, he decided to return for a time to the town in which he'd spent his youth. He had no family in this place, nor friends he wished to contact. He simply felt the need to reconnect, in some small way, with the last thing in his life that had made sense. His adulthood, so it now appeared, had consisted of little more than self-deception. He had built his petite kingdom around a gaping void, and now the void had come to claim its bounty.

Albin was scarcely acknowledged by the man behind the counter as he approached the ticket booth. A single folded banknote secured his admission to the manor in which, presumably, the missing sovereign would be found. The man motioned with his eyes toward the carriages as he pushed a paper slip beneath the gap in the window. Albin took the small pink rectangle which he supposed comprised his ticket. He was unsure why he needed it or to whom he might present it. Flipping it over in his fingers, he puzzled at the image on the back: an unfurling whip careened across the length of the paper, its leather handle held suspended in the air as if by an invisible hand. Curious, he slipped the useless item into one of the many pockets of his overcoat.

The transaction marked the first faint hope, however fleeting, that the depressive torpor which had taken hold of him might at last be overcome. The attraction he was about to enter was no less than a relic. At one time, nearly every minor city in the country featured an institution of this type. They had been the result of a passing trend, and when their time had come they simply disappeared, replaced by reptile petting zoos or milk bars or whatever it was that had come into fashion next.

Albin had been particularly fond of the local mystery house when he was younger. It had always struck him as superior to the others that he'd visited. He couldn't quite remember exactly where it had been located. It may have been somewhere just outside of the commercial district, though the precise street eluded him. He strained to recall its title as he headed toward the empty carriage. It was comprised of a short phrase if he remembered correctly—*The Chamber of the Night Flower*, or perhaps *The Flower in the Night Chamber*.

As with others of its type, little more than the price of a newspaper would buy a trip through the interior of the house. A mystery was presented, perhaps several mysteries all intertwined. There were clues, red herrings, and intricate narrative twists. Albin had undergone the experience innumerable times, taking in every detail with a careful eye. He'd mapped out the layout with pencil and paper and made complex diagrams to keep track of all the subtexts. No effort was spared to examine the significance of the drama presented before him. So complex and subtle were the insinuations that he invariably became overwhelmed. His fascination with the ride had left a mark upon him. The narratives it offered, while he could scarcely comprehend them, held the promise of a lifetime's worth of exploration. It was precisely this which had kept him coming back.

He had always been fiendishly clever. His father, who had run a modest imports business, would frequently bring back gifts from such places as China, Indonesia, Thailand, and Morocco. Tangrams, sliding block puzzles, interlocking burr toys and other classic amusements found their way into Albin's insatiable hands. Diversions of this type were a poor substitute for the fatherly affection that had largely been denied him, yet they captivated his imagination and engendered within him an unquenchable thirst for the abstruse. As the years passed, his interests developed into an obsession with philosophical conundrums and paradoxes. He devoured detective stories and locked room mysteries, studied the mechanics of abstract strategical games, and scrutinized the ambiguities of esoteric manuscripts found languishing in libraries and archives. His young mind luxuriated in the rarified fires of mystification and obscurity.

Later in life, having embarked on a career in the world of academia, he turned his attention to cognitive science, semiotics, and taxonomy. From the ashes of past disciplines, he synthesized new models by which color and music might be more efficiently utilized. He published several highly regarded papers, including an inspired study on syncsthesia, and yet his reputation, still so young, could not withstand the ravages of the defamation that would inevitably come when he upset the wrong people. He was perplexed by the political machinations of an elite that he had no ability to understand. He found himself on the wrong side of several arbitrary boundaries without the slightest idea how he might atone for his unwitting transgressions. Strings were pulled, loyalties were shifted, doors which had been opened for him were abruptly closed again. His wife, as it turned out, was married not to him, but to the promise of a seat among an unofficial aristocracy. He quickly came to realize that he had no place among these people. It was as if his very blood were tainted.

Having washed up on the sordid shores of ignominy and ruin, he sought in vain for a lost innocence that had never truly existed. Thus he wandered through the darkening streets of the city of his youth like a minister who'd misplaced the sacraments. The link to his past that had unexpectedly appeared to him was somewhat of a godsend. Having already drunk in earnest from the waters of despair, he would consume his nostalgia like an opiate.

Albin took his place in one of the carriages beneath the arch. The car was suffused with the scent of old leather. Two short doors, the handles of which were nearly rusted shut, allowed entrance on either side. A black canopy extended over the top of the vehicle, while the sides and front remained open.

The track to which the carriage was affixed passed behind the ticket booth and through an open doorway. Beyond that point, the route curved sharply to the left. Albin sat in the carriage for a minute or two, not entirely certain that the ride was in proper operating condition. Perhaps this was all that would be permitted to him—he'd sit in place for several minutes then simply get up and walk away.

As if to spite his disappointment, the mechanism lurched into operation. A sound like the release of steam from a furnace filled the chamber, followed by the escalating whine of an unfathomable engine. A thrill ran along Albin's spine as the car jerked forward and proceeded, ever so slowly, toward the doorway ahead. The monotonous clacking of the wheels in their iron grooves was as familiar to him as the moon. The carriage moved through the open entrance and around the bend, pulled along by belts and chains that were hidden from sight. For the first time in months, he felt alive again.

He passed beneath a marble archway illuminated by a flaming lamp that hung suspended from a chain. Without warning, the track dipped and Albin was plunged into darkness. The churning and groaning of belts, gears, and pulleys echoed throughout the hollows of the mechanical contrivance. It sounded as if the carriage were submerged in the bowels of an ancient, infernal machine. The wheeze of compressed air contended with the clacking of flywheels and the desperate gasp of pistons. The noise was accentuated by the relative blindness to which Albin had suddenly been subjected. Traces of light streamed in from above and behind, illuminating little more than the contours of the walls. It was not uncommon for rides of this type to subject the passenger to brief periods of darkness, though never for long enough to allow the eyes to adjust to the low level of light.

The carriage rounded a sharp corner and emerged before an elaborate display bathed in the soft light of a chandelier. Here the wheels slowly came to a halt. Albin looked out onto an extravagant study decorated in a self-consciously Victorian style. The room was separated from the track by a red velvet rope held in place by metal poles. Wood-paneled walls enclosed an open area of modest dimensions. The walls were lined with sunken bookshelves filled with leather-bound volumes and white marble busts. Behind a heavy wooden writing desk that occupied one corner sat a human figure immersed in study. A hefty tome lay open amidst the stacks of books and papers which were meticulously arranged upon the surface of the desk.

The figure was dressed in such extravagant finery as to suggest a hint of the absurd. The stiffness of his posture made it clear to Albin that he was looking at an automated mannequin. The use of automatons was common to these productions, which borrowed heavily from theater. The early mystery houses had made use of live actors, but the cost was generally prohibitive while simply constructed automatons were relatively cheap and required little upkeep. The face of the figure behind the desk was remarkably life-like, with its well-trimmed beard and head of thick, brown hair. The rigidity of the features was a necessary limitation—no matter how skillful the creator, it remained impossible to craft a doll that possessed the precise range of expression unique to humans. Thus were the automatons forced to rely on grand gestures in order to convey even the most basic of emotions.

With a sigh of hidden gears, the figure shifted into motion. His head rose from his studies, the chair rolled back, and he rose with stilted movements. A high-pitched wail of mechanical ennui accompanied his movement to the center of the floor. The logistics of walking were far beyond the capacity of automatons such as this one. They tended rather to glide from place to place along tracks set into the floor in much the same way as did the carriages. Indeed, several pairs of tracks could be seen crisscrossing the otherwise elegant carpet of the study.

Upon reaching center stage, the lifeless doll affected a swift change in position. One arm rose with inhuman stiffness to the violet buttons of the silken vest while the other extended away from the body, palm up with the fingers remaining closely pressed together. The head jerked back with an awkward twinge, the light resting gently on the contours of the face. A resonant voice piped through a speaker that seemed to be located somewhere behind Albin's right shoulder.

"These mysteries beguile and vex my very soul," the doll appeared to say. "I am compelled to seek the lost word of the Freemasons, the secrets of the ancient oracles, the enigmas of the prophets, and the dimensions of the vaults of heaven, and yet my grasping hand encloses only dust and shadows. I have searched through the ruins of shattered temples and have scoured the remnants of their altars. I've braved the desert wastes that I might behold the seraphim—and yet, as in all things, I have failed. I'm plagued with an insatiable thirst for hidden truth and revelation, yet each time I draw near to my goal I'm denied entrance to the sanctuary. Still, I follow the wisdom of the sages in the hope that some forgotten god might wake me from my slumber. My torch remains aflame in the thick darkness of the night. I am driven by powerful urges that I can neither explain nor understand."

A brief pause in the action allowed Albin to shift his position in the carriage. Turning to one side, he leaned forward and rested against the side door facing the stage. The doll remained in a fixed position, as if petrified by his very yearnings. The illusion of life was unconvincing—the figure resembled nothing more than a well-dressed object.

The door behind the automaton suddenly swung open as if blown by a meandering wind. A second mannequin glided in along the tracks set into the carpet—a woman in a stunning dress of pearl replete with ruffled lace. A head of rich, blonde hair framed an affable face affected with a hint of irony. Her arms and hands were positioned such that she appeared to be engaged in a perpetual dance. A female voice echoed slightly through the open space as the woman's figure approached that of the scholar. "How fare you, young Tresler?" Her question betrayed a slight edge of contempt at which the figure of the man seemed almost to recoil.

Tresler turned to face the woman, arms remaining in position. "Do you come again to mock me, Agrippina? Is my disquiet not enough for you? Must you exacerbate my suffering with the sting of your contempt?"

"Does not suffering exalt the soul?" she said, her head slightly bowing. "What might I bring to aid you? A pocketful of blasphemy? A whispered sacrilege? A rumor of dissent among the initiated brethren? Or will my disdain alone inspire your little house of cards to come pitiably crashing to the floor?" Everything about this woman seemed designed to ridicule her adversary, though always with a certain restraint. The understatement of her movements seemed only to add weight to the insulting tone of her speech. Albin wasn't sure that he'd ever seen such masterful handling in an automaton before.

"I assure you, Agrippina, that my studies are quite serious." Tresler remained motionless, his voice scarcely connected to his body. "I seek no less than the ever-burning flame of the mysteries of the ancients."

"Take care, lest the flame consume your beloved books," said Agrippina, turning her back with a nonchalance that bordered on malice. "May I suggest, as well, that you seek in the wrong place? Your inquiries neglect what lies directly before you. Have you forgotten that this very house holds mysteries worthy of consideration? There are doors here, I can assure you, for which you don't possess the keys."

"This is none of my concern," replied Tresler, the inconsistent murmur of mechanical motion accompanying his retreat back toward the writing desk. "Your contemptuous games only spur me on to greater immersion in my studies. This house is old and dusty and not worth exploring. The attics are given to mold and rot and the cellars are partial to flooding in the winter. I renounce my heritage of whatever heirlooms might be locked away in one room or another. Such transient concerns are simply not for me."

"Do you renounce the house along with the heirlooms?" Agrippina turned and pursued her companion, placing her arms around his shoulders from behind. Albin couldn't help but notice that the hum which accompanied her movement along the rails seemed more refined than Tresler's, nearly delicate. "And what about the master?" her recorded voice continued. "Where, young Tresler, is the master of the house? Is he locked in the attic or lost in the cellar? Where, oh where, might he be found?"

"There is no master of this house," he said, a hint of regret in his voice.

"And what of your father?" Agrippina laid her head on Tresler's shoulder.

"My father is dead," he said softly.

"Perhaps you are mistaken," she said. "The dead have a way of resurrecting themselves where we least expect them to. After all, a house cannot abide without a master, can it? No more than can a country prosper in the absence of a sovereign."

Tresler broke from her embrace with a clumsy jerk, gliding to the other side of the study. His arms remained in the exact same position they'd assumed when he rose from the desk. Agrippina turned toward him, hands held before her like autumn leaves. "Perhaps your brother Klein could tell us where the sovereign of this woebegotten country might be found," she proposed.

"I grow tired of your games, Agrippina." Tresler turned away from her to face the bookshelves. "I am a busy man. Leave me to my studies."

"Fare thee well then, my studious friend." Agrippina drifted back toward the door. "May the fruits of your labors return to you like falcons with doves held in their beaks." She passed through the exit and the door closed behind her.

Tresler proceeded to the writing desk with a rigidity befitting his character. His hands dropped to its surface with an unruly clatter as he sunk back into the chair. "The master of the house, indeed!" he lamented beneath the dim light of the chandelier.

With a slight jerk and a whining heave of gears, the carriage again stirred into motion. Albin found himself unexpectedly cheered as he was plunged once more into darkness. The restrained motion of the mannequins, the poor quality of the voice-acting, the very shades and textures of the set designs recalled to him something of the flavor of his young adulthood. He recalled a notebook, long since lost, in which he'd compiled an impressive list of clues, each of them revealing hidden aspects of the themes revealed to him in the local mystery house. The peeling back of one layer of the enigma never failed to reveal yet another. The depths of the mystery had seemed endless to him at the time.

The carriage rounded a corner and began a gradual ascent. The familiar scent of well-oiled iron and polished wood suffused the darkened space. Albin felt almost as if he was young again, so potently did the long-forgotten sensations move him. The soul partakes of substances and essences, so he considered, that we scarcely have the capacity to retain. They slip between our fingers only to reappear as fleeting reflections in the mirror of the distant past. He found himself wondering if these phantoms of memory were more significant than the events that inspired them.

He emerged from his reverie just as a glimmer of light appeared in the distance ahead. Within seconds, the carriage had come to rest before a fancy drawing room. A marble fireplace contended with a rich array of furniture, all upholstered in vibrant shades of red and yellow. Again the scene was partitioned from the track by a rope of red velvet.

Here Agrippina shared the scene with a different figure, a man no less distinguished than Tresler. She sat on a divan before a large, full-length mirror, the elegance of her bearing tinged with the poison of contempt. The other man stood near the fireplace. He wore a long, grey overcoat and gripped a polished wooden cane in one hand. He appeared to study a row of photographs that stood lined up on the mantelpiece. The cut of his beard, painted directly onto his face, differed slightly from that of Tresler's. Otherwise, his facial features were more or less the same. This must be Klein, thought Albin.

"The coin of the realm has been insufferably tarnished," uttered the mechanical man. He turned to face Agrippina in the light of a pair of lamps that were mounted to the wall above the marble ledge. "Indeed, the entire house has fallen into disgrace. We, who were once so lofty, have become mere servants. We've lost our family name, our purpose, and our dignity—the thread by which our ancestors had so deftly navigated history have led us into a cul-de-sac. We scarcely even know the heights from which we've fallen." Klein's body rotated ever so slightly so that he faced the carriage. "It would seem that we are truly lost."

"You give up far too easily, young Klein," said Agrippina. The upper half of her body reclined on the divan, while her legs, both of a single piece, remained rooted to the track set into the floor. "Nothing has been lost that cannot be re-invented. Your problem is that, while ambition is not wanting, you have little vision and no courage."

"I have every intention of scaling the heights that lie so dauntingly before me," said Klein as he turned toward Agrippina, his cane tightly gripped in one inflexible hand. "Yet I must take care to do so without disgracing our lineage. I won't indulge in the sort of transgressions which you seem to have adopted as virtue. Honestly, Agrippina! You trespass into places that have been forbidden to you, pilfering and rearranging as you please. Your penchant for gossip has cheapened what little virtue this house might still possess. You have a way of stoking fires which ought to have been put out ages ago."

"I simply follow the dictates of an authority which is immeasurably higher than your own," said Agrippina as she rose amidst the soft glow of the wall-mounted lamps. "I keep watch over a hidden flame. There's vitality in the fires that I tend, however much you refuse to acknowledge it."

"You've implicated yourself among our ranks, yet you know damn well that you're not one of us," continued Klein. "You're like the vermin that infects the crops—once you've made your nest, there's no getting rid of you."

"My blood runs through the hidden veins and arteries of this house." She approached her opponent, her hands trailing gently behind her as she moved. "If I were to leave this place, the supporting structure would collapse. Is this what you would have of me?"

"What I would have of you," he uttered softly, "is your complicity. I would be the master of the house."

"You'll never be the master of this house," she insisted as she sailed back toward the divan. "The old master is still with us."

Klein again turned toward the mantlepiece. Agrippina lowered herself back onto the divan with her chin slightly raised in the air. Her reclining figure, where it was concealed by her dress, could almost have been alive. She seemed to have a presence, to be animated by a subtle air which resided in the hollows of her mechanical sheath. For all of that, there was no question that she was definitely an automaton, if one of exceeding finesse.

For the first time, Albin noticed a large, gold-framed painting hanging on the wall behind the divan. The piece was larger than either of the mannequins, Klein being slightly taller than Agrippina. The image blended perfectly with the surrounding décor. Dull charcoal, rich brown, ebony, and umber dominated a landscape in which a tumultuous windstorm assailed a dense copse of trees. A whirlwind of branches, leaves, and torn cloth careened in rapturous arcs around the body of a tremendous mule. The latter stood partially hidden in the shadows, its face illuminated from one side. A silver crown gleamed from the top of its head while two glaring eyes peered out like penetrating diamonds.

A detail in one corner of the painting caught Albin's attention. It appeared at first to be nothing more than a scrap of white cloth fluttering in the wind near the feet of the crowned beast. On closer inspection, the shape revealed a human figure, one arm raised in greeting or salute, his back turned to the viewer as he faced the darkness of the desolate wood beyond. The mule seemed to tower above the piteous figure—or perhaps the robed personage was standing some distance behind it. The perspective was skewed in such a way that Albin found it difficult to tell. Further, the mule wore an expression which struck him as distinctly preposterous. A slight curling of the lip lent it an almost human aspect. The beast thus conveyed a knowing malice, as if it had conspired with the winds to bring about some baleful accident that could not be discerned by the viewer.

Albin's attention was again drawn to Agrippina, who had risen to a sitting position. "Nature devours those who seek her hidden treasures but are too timid to take them," she said with teasing eyes. "If you can't be the master of the house, you could at least rise within its ranks. You might attain some measure of prestige, had you the heart for it. The only thing that stands in your way is your inability to act. You know what must be done, yet you cannot force your hand to do it."

Klein turned to face her, one hand clutching the cane as if with an iron grip. "I must not act rashly," he said. "Everything must take place in its proper time. The hour for action has not yet come, is all."

"Do it now," taunted Agrippina, her face a mask of disdain, her upright torso supported by her lithe white arms as her palms rested on the upholstery. "Why wait for what is inevitable?"

"I may be a servant in my own house," replied Klein, a hint of agitation in his voice, "but I am not your servant."

Agrippina rose. "You must not allow Tresler to stand in your way any longer." She moved with an uncanny grace toward Klein, taking her place behind him. She lowered her head and gently whispered in his ear: "Kill him!"

"Get ahold of yourself!" shouted Klein, distancing himself from the derisive woman. "You only make yourself look foolish with your games and provocations." He stood now near the divan.

"Do it, Klein," she persisted as she slowly moved toward him.

"Damn you, Agrippina! I'm warning you." He raised his cane before him as if to defend himself against her advances. His disembodied voice rose just above the capacity of the sound system, giving rise to a faint, short burst of static.

Agrippina's arms shot above her head. Quickly and with great mechanical force, she spun three times in place as if performing a spasmodic pirouette. "KILL HIM! KILL HIM! KILL HIM!" With the final spin, she landed upon the edge of the divan in a fit of delicious laughter.

"Will you keep your voice down!" hissed Klein. "Have you lost your mind?"

Agrippina's laughter trailed off. She raised her head toward her adversary. "Shall I get my sister to do it for you?"

"I don't want to hear a single word about your sister," said Klein. "Not now, not ever. Do you understand? I've had enough."

"I can fetch her for you," she said. "Would you like that? She is quite enamored of you."

"Shut up, Agrippina," Klein's voice had regained some measure of calm. "Just shut up."

"I can bring her through the mirror." One arm rose in a gesture toward the tall glass. "That's part of the bargain we keep between us. I can go in and she can come out."

Klein remained silent, turning toward the wall.

"I can see her coming now." Her eyes seemed to shift toward the mirror. "She must have heard us talking about her. Here she comes..."

"Damn your sister!" shouted Klein as he turned and raised his cane above his head. With one swift slash, he brought the stick down on the mirror's surface. A minor explosion followed. Shards of glass went sailing through the air, landing on the floor and the divan, showering the mantlepiece, crashing on the tracks and even within the carriage itself. Albin was shocked to find several broken fragments in his lap and on the seat next to him.

Agrippina began again with her maniacal laughter. The carriage had already begun to move on as if, sensitive to the very real danger presented, it was urged to enact a tactical retreat. Agrippina's cackling echoed through the chamber. "You fool," she could be heard to say as Albin was again submerged in darkness. "You utter fool!"

Albin carefully brushed the broken glass from his overcoat. He could only assume that he had witnessed a mechanical malfunction. Klein's arm must have fallen beneath its own weight, bringing the cane into forceful contact with the glass while it had been intended to stop just short of striking the surface. It was not entirely uncommon for the mechanics of these old attractions to go awry in one way or another—Albin had seen mannequins get stuck on the rails and heard voice recordings go out of sync with the action. The shattering glass was the most dramatic incident he'd witnessed. It was rather unfortunate, as the mirror must be costly and would doubtless have to be replaced.

The carriage once again continued its ascent, curving ever to the left through the dark corridors of the house. Occasional patches of light could be seen in the distance, affording fleeting glimpses of other rooms replete with lavish ornamentation. Specific details were impossible to make out. All that could be seen was an occasional flash of candlelight. The distant echo of metal on metal vied with the moderate cacophony arising from the carriage to form a richly textured ambiance as melodic as it was disorienting. Albin closed his eyes for a moment, letting the harmonies and discords cascade through the caverns of his body.

Opening his eyes again, he began to ponder the mysteries thus far presented to him. On the one hand, he'd been left with the distinct impression that

Agrippina was meant to appear younger than either of the two brothers, yet he couldn't quite shake the notion that there was something ancient about her. It had been hinted that her roots, perhaps stretching far into the distant past, were deeply entangled with those of Kline and Tresler. He wondered how, precisely, she'd become involved with the household. It was clear that she was not exactly one of them.

His ruminations were cut short by a sudden change of scenery. The dim glow of a chandelier shed light on his surroundings as the carriage slowed. His ride came to a stop before a pair of curving stairways which rose to a landing above. A central doorway sat nestled between the bases of the stairs, above which hung a circular mirror in a frame of polished brass or copper, its surface slightly convex and entirely dark. The upper landing was concealed by a balustrade of rich, dark wood. Two further doors stood on either side on the current floor. Opposite the scene, on his right side, one of the tall, arched windows that could be seen from the outside of the building towered above him, the dim glow of moonlight refracted through its panes. As with the two previous displays, a rope divider stood between the presentation and the tracks, though this time the divider lay open in the middle.

Albin paused before the empty display, unsure as to whether he was waiting for another character to make their entrance. As before, tracks could be seen running along the carpet behind the ropes. Rails ran atop the stairs to allow for the ascent and descent of automatons. It seemed quite possible that the scene was to be populated, that another segment of the drama would be played out before him. On the other hand, perhaps he was expected to leave the carriage and venture further into the house on foot. Albin would have thought that a sign would be appropriate, or some other means by which the passenger might be informed of the proper course of action. Of course, that wouldn't really fit with the sophistication of this particular ride. The ambiguity, the evocation of uncertainty, was most probably intentional.

Several minutes passed during which Albin was paralyzed with indecision. He'd hate to be responsible for a breach of protocol. The prospect of eliciting the scorn of the ticket-seller didn't sit at all well with him. He'd always been uneasy with conflict of any sort. Disapproval triggered long-standing feelings of inadequacy, usually accompanied by an overwhelming desire to simply disappear. Already he was flushed with irrational guilt. The simple appearance of an ambiguous choice was enough to make him feel that his existence was erroneous. At last he decided, with a mixture of exasperation and spite, to defy the silence and step out of the carriage.

He spared a quick glance at the floor, checking to ensure that there was no external rail on which he might accidentally electrocute himself. He got out, stood up, and brushed the remaining slivers of glass from his overcoat. Placing both hands on the edge of the stage (why was there no stair?), he hoisted himself up and scrambled quickly to his feet.

The three lower doors were all tightly closed. He suspected that they wouldn't open if he tried them. In any case, it seemed quite clear that the intended route involved the landing above. Which of the two stairways would it be best to take, he wondered? He placed a hand upon the railing of the stairway to the left. The sensation of bare wood beneath his fingertips brought with it a return to physicality. He'd let himself retreat into his thoughts as the carriage had taken him from place to place. Feeling that he was crossing a definite boundary, he slowly began his ascent. He'd nearly reached the upper landing when a loud click rang through the hall, followed by the echo of a mechanical groan. Horrified, he quickly turned around, half-convinced that the carriage was beginning its journey to the next station without him. Fully prepared to leap back down the stairs and dive into the coach, he was relieved to see that the cart was still in place. He remained frozen on the stair for a moment, watching the carriage for the slightest hint of motion. He wondered if the noise had been intentionally produced to startle him. After another moment, nerves on edge, he turned and resumed his ascent.

The upper landing was suffused in the soft radiance of the bare bulbs on the chandelier. This blended with the warm glow of two wall-mounted lamps to produce a mild and pleasing ambiance. The dark reds of the carpet, the gold and yellow of the flowered wallpaper, and the rich wood of the balustrade were made to blossom in the gentle light. The pleasing character of the décor was offset by just a hint of neglect. The wallpaper was clearly peeling in a couple of places. The carpet was slightly worn, especially in those areas in which the rails were set. A sizable crack appeared in the plaster in one section of the ceiling. To Albin's left lay an unlit hallway, as uninviting an avenue as he could possibly hope for. A staircase ascended to the right into what looked to be a reasonably well-lit area. His path forward was clear.

Again, he was disarmed by an unexpected noise. This time it was the soft hum which had accompanied the movements of the mannequins in the previous scenes. From the pitch and timbre of the drone, he felt quite certain that he was hearing Agrippina's passage along one of the rails above. Her's had an almost musical quality about it, quite in contrast to the coarse vibration produced by the other mannequins. Feeling much more confident about his passage through the house, Albin made his way up the stairs in the hope of viewing the next dramatic act.

He emerged into a spacious chamber lined with bookshelves and lit by a single standing lamp. The bulb was shaded with red and white fabric that cast multi-colored shadows on the spines of several tattered volumes. Agrippina stood before one of the shelves, her back turned to Albin as she appeared to scrutinize a row of titles. A soft, golden light suffused with particles of dust shone through an archway in a wall of dark wood. A hint of decay suffused this upper level, the air tinged with a sweetness vaguely redolent of rotting amber.

Albin paused at the head of the stairs, unsure how best to proceed. It seemed absurd to feel slighted by a senseless automaton, yet he couldn't shake the feeling that he was being ignored. Several seconds passed before the figure turned to face him. Where Klein and Tressler were constructed in a way that allowed for jarring, inelegant rotation, this particular model could pivot with remarkable grace. Her gaze, if you could call it as much, looked through him rather than at him, yet nonetheless imparted the illusion of sentience. Her stance, her bearing, and the way in which she held her arms all betrayed a faint suggestion of superiority. Albin could almost make himself believe that she felt genuine contempt for him.

A voice streamed in from somewhere above, startling Albin nearly out of his skin. "I must compliment you on your impudence," it said. "You are like a little cockroach, scampering along into the upper reaches of the house without a guide. It's not often that our guests demonstrate such audacity. I suppose there's something to admire in it." She turned back to the bookshelf where, with a graceful movement of one arm, she pushed a protruding volume into place. A brief pause followed before she turned again to face her visitor. "While you're here, I may as well take you on a tour of the attics," the recorded voice continued. "You may call me Phrygia, if you call me anything at all. Most of our guests are so abysmally boorish. You would think their tongues were made of lead."

Albin kept silent, unable to bring himself to respond to what was no more than a cleverly orchestrated mechanical device. Common sense notwithstanding, he found it difficult to meet her gaze. He felt a pang of self-consciousness, as if he were being observed. Wishing he could put his apprehensions to one side, he simply waited for his hostess to resume her role, his passivity justified only by the fact that he had paid to undergo this experience.

He wondered, as he waited, at the change of the character's name. Was this intended to be the same personage that had appeared in the two previous scenes? It seemed entirely possible that the pretense of deception was a deliberate part of the act. He had little time to think it through before she turned herself around again and headed along a weathered rail beneath the shadow of the archway. "Come along, my little cockroach," she gently teased. "I'll show you things you've never seen before."

Albin followed his hostess into a long and expansive chamber, the further end of which was hidden behind a cascading assemblage of half-empty bookshelves. Several doors opened up into further reaches of the house while others remained tightly closed. The walls and ceiling, which rose some distance from the floor, were comprised of rough panels of unpainted wood. The complete lack of windows gave the impression that they were somewhere in the heart of the structure. Sporadic lamps and overhead bulbs cast a tapestry of shadows before cabinets, dressers, full-length mirrors, and the occasional divan. The floor was largely covered in a patchwork of carpets, ornate yet for the most part threadbare. A perplexing network of sunken rails traced elaborate curves along the floor, continuing beneath closed doors and sometimes even curving back into themselves.

Phrygia followed the rails to an ostentatious cabinet fronted with several rows of ornate knobs and handles. Albin attempted to determine, as he trailed in her wake, whether the soft whir of her motor was subtly different from that of Agrippina's. She stopped before the cabinet and turned to an angle that concealed one side of her face. Her voice seemed to emerge from a speaker concealed somewhere high above. "Your leaden tongue might be forgiven, considering the circumstances. I myself have been accused of having a heart of rust and glass. We all have our innate deficiencies." She turned her body toward him. "We're constructed from a template that no longer suits us and we stumble, as if drunken, through a house we fail to recognize as our own. We can't even be certain whether the house has a master. We're not so different, you and I." She paused once more, turning again to one side.

"I am aware how we must look to you." The voice was punctuated, ever so faintly, by the distant clang and flutter of machinery. "Our guests undoubtedly think us depraved. We play our games and we tally scores that are meaningless to anyone but ourselves, acting out intrigues and taking on roles that are partially concealed and partly in the light."

She turned again to face the cabinet. It was larger than a standard Victorian model, being several arm-lengths wide. A long, polished surface stood below three pairs of doors, each inset with plates of copper etched with an intricate floral pattern. Behind the central pair, which stood wide open, were six rows of drawers, each one fit with a tiny handle.

"I have something for you," the voice continued. "You can consider it a gift. It may be useful to you later on."

She lifted an arm before one of the drawers, a smooth sweep which, in its lack of flexibility, readily demonstrated her doll-like nature. She moved her body a few inches forward, causing her fingertips to strike the drawer with a delicate tap. "In here," she said softly, moving slightly to one side, just enough to allow Albin to approach the cabinet.

Albin had allowed himself to become lost in the performance. It took him a moment to realize that he was expected to respond. He wondered what might happen if he were simply to walk away. Would the scene continue if he was no longer present, or might the technology behind the house be sophisticated enough to respond to his abdication?

Whatever the case may be, he had no desire to act against his given role. He approached the cabinet, pulled the indicated drawer, and removed from its recesses a small white coin, taking a moment to examine it in the dim light from overhead. He could not quite ascertain the metal from which the coin was forged. It looked vaguely like aluminum, but it was much too heavy. Perhaps it was some kind of alloy. A face in profile was embossed into the surface on one side, its features bearing a startling likeness to his own. The august personage, crowned and dignified, looked far more regal than did he, yet the resemblance was surprising.

Turning the coin over, the other side revealed the figure of a horse. Albin thought of the English sovereign coin, the back side of which featured a depiction of St. George on horseback, presumably on his way to battle the fabled dragon. "The ivory sovereign, indeed," he thought, running his front two fingers over the body of the beast. Something about the notion of the horse without a rider caused him discomfort. It was as if he was looking at a pornographic image. The figure presented a shameless display of animal essence, raw and untamed. Somehow, it made him feel indecently exposed. Wishing to conceal the item safely out of sight, he placed it in an inside pocket of his overcoat.

"It belongs to my sister," said Phrygia, with her usual impeccable timing. She still faced away from him, as if ashamed to look at him directly. "Or at least it used to before I got my hands on it. She'll be furious when she discovers its absence." The mannequin turned again to face her guest. "Stolen items are endowed with special properties, don't you think? They have a unique power all their own. They've crossed over a boundary and they carry with them every sort of trouble, yet the advantage afforded to those who possess them is well worth the risk." Her face was masked in a violet veil of lightly-textured shadow. Albin could swear he sensed a hint of perfume about her—sandalwood, musk, or something equally seductive. She continued, her resonant voice accompanied by the hiss of the magnetic tape. "What might be purchased with a stolen coin which cannot be had by other means?"

For the first time, Albin looked his hostess in the eye. An empty, lifeless mask looked back at him. He tried to put aside the persistent notion that she was simply hiding from him behind a pretense of automatism. Anxious to continue, he stepped away from the cabinet.

"My sister was once very dear to me," said Phrygia with a hint of melancholy. "I'm afraid we've fallen on difficult times. She's crossed over to the other side now. I'll not see her for some time to come. This house imposes limitations on us all, I suppose." She turned and retraced her path with an elegance befitting a member of a household in high standing. At last she came to a point upon the floor on which several of the rails intersected.

"Come along, cockroach," she said in a tone not entirely lacking in affection, swiftly gliding along a sinuous route which led them further into the attic. "Deeper, ever deeper into the bowels of the house we go. There are chambers concealed in this infernal mansion that harbor secrets that are truly terrible. I'll try and spare you the disgraces of our past. There's hardly any need for you to look upon our shame. For you, a vision of the glimmer of the crown, if only seen in reflection."

Between a sturdy wardrobe and a row of cabinets they proceeded, Albin following dutifully behind his high-bred host. The distant creak and grind of machines resounded with a hollow echo as they continued. They passed through a succession of tight enclosures delineated by large wooden panels. Decorative shoji screens passed them by, along with sliding bookshelves attached to rafters, hanging silks, and other fabrics. The further they ventured, the more the space seemed to extend, spanning distances which seemed to exceed the capacity of the containing building.

"Ancient artifacts abound here in the attics," said Phrygia as they passed a grand piano draped in intricate lacework. "This house is littered with the detritus of intrigues that reach back through the mists of distant memory. Just as a painted image may present the illusion of depth, so the veil of history is deceptive. The mirror of the past conceals relics of great power, yet we overlook them in our efforts to reconstruct something we've never lost. The scattered remnants of a fallen empire lie nearly in our grasp, and yet..." She stopped before a silken curtain of deep amber which hung before an arch, effectively concealing the chamber that lay beyond. She turned, after a moment of hesitation, to face Albin. Her eyes were concealed by shadows cast by the shimmering flames of a nearby candelabra. She appeared nearly human in the flickering light. He could almost have embraced her. "Tell me, cockroach," she gently provoked him. "Would you hold court with the eternal? Would you renounce the specter of your past? Would you pierce the shimmering veil that so seduces the nostalgic?"

She turned toward the archway, a delicate pivot which almost assuaged the sting of Albin's discomfort. He chided himself for the guilt he felt at his inability to respond. It was nearly as difficult for him to ignore her as it would have been to speak to her aloud.

Her body glided smoothly past the amber veil, forcing it to yield in her wake. Albin followed, brushing the curtain to one side. They entered a long chamber bordered with several closed doors. The floor was covered with dark stone tiles with a series of arches painted onto their surfaces—two rows of three each. Their angles and perspectives were somewhat crude, as if slightly, inconsistently, exaggerated. Each of them harbored the figure of a woman painted in chalky white with dark, bold outlines. Their faces were fraught with the austerity adopted by those who know too much. Each cradled an open book in one arm while their free hand clutched an implement. One figure held a whip, another a crown of thorns, a third an ink brush suspended above a sheet of parchment. There was also a dove, an upturned horn, and a banner that fluttered in the wind. The curves traced by the rails set into the tiles added definition to the figures and their implements. Their winding paths, which crossed over one another like the leaves and shoots of conjoined flowers, continued onward to the far end of the room.

"My sisters, my beautiful sisters, my own flesh and blood," sighed Phrygia as she glided with a dismal grace among the time-worn images. "Nearly all of them are lost to me. There are several others who are not pictured here. I don't think I could name them all from memory. We've scattered to the winds, fleeing to the ends of the earth in search of remnants of the stone that once bound us. Our efforts are fruitless. The stone has been shattered." Pools of light and shadow cast by the wall-mounted candles danced in graceful waves across her body as she moved among the images. "Here is Erythrea composing her beloved acrostics, and Tiburtina, and Cumana." Albin could scarcely keep track of which of the figures she was indicating as she named them, such was the rapidity with which she navigated the curving paths. "I myself am pictured here," she continued. "Along with Delphica with the horn and little Agrippina with her whip. She is with me still, Agrippina, though she's not inclined to walk with me. We've had," she paused. "...disagreements. An arrangement has been made between us. I have not found it satisfactory."

Albin followed his mechanical guide to the other side of the room, taking care to step around the pale images of Phrygia and her sisters. A slab of white marble was affixed to the far wall by heavy, golden clasps. Two vibrant flames arose from slender tapers in tall, black stands to either side. Albin wondered for the first time who it was that kept the candles lit. He imagined it must be necessary to change them when they burned down. They illuminated an image carved in relief upon the slab, a depiction of a figure at once magnificent and ominous. She stood above a throne set in a circle of stone pillars, her torso thrown forward as if to assail an advancing army. A fragment of cloth enwrapped her glorious body. One arm was stretched out before her. Her brow was crossed with a portentous fire that bespoke unmitigated catastrophe. The expression on her face could cause an empire to combust. "Our antecedent," said Phrygia, as she sailed in a graceful curve between Albin and one of the open archways. "The mother of prophecy and the spirit of necessity—she, at least, is still with me."

He stepped closer to the image to examine it more carefully. Several men were pictured outside the pillars, though they were hardly noticeable for the sheer enormity of the woman. They abided in fields of golden wheat. Some of them had fallen to their knees as if stricken down or afflicted. Others had turned their backs to her, unable to bear the weight of her rancor. "I can call her before us if you'd like," said Phrygia. "Though I'm afraid it won't be possible for you to meet her face-to-face."

Above the marble slab hung a dark, circular mirror set into a copper frame, much like the one that Albin had noticed when he'd disembarked from the carriage. The convexity of the polished glass lent a deficiency to the piece, its black surface suggesting a void that demanded fulfillment. He was unable to dismiss the notion that the two mirrors were somehow connected.

The mechanical timbre of Phrygia's voice issued forth from behind him with an uneven cadence. It almost sounded as if her gears were slightly out of joint. "Hail, oh guardians of the pivot, wardens of immutable flame," she proceeded, "who turn at one command the revolving axis of the vault of heaven." Albin turned around to see her arms raised before her as if heralding the approach of royalty. The flickering radiance of the candlelight caressed the plastic coating on her hands and face. He felt the unmistakable sensation of another presence in the room, much larger than that of his insentient companion. "But what on earth could you possibly...?" he began before his muttering was silenced by the voice of his hostess.

"Come forth, oh hand of fate unwavering, living and unliving," she continued. "Iron rod of destiny, mother of the past and of the time to come." The incantation was given to an infernal musicality. Phrygia's body seemed to wave and fluctuate as if gently buffeted by mysterious winds. A high-pitched buzzing pervaded the room, far subtler and more penetrant than the distant hum of the machines. It seemed to infiltrate the recesses of Albin's body and violate his heart. "Come to me—your daughter," the automaton continued. "Come by names forgotten and obscured. I await you with affection in your consecrated court."

Albin turned again toward the graven image. A cold sweat had overtaken him. He wavered on the precarious line between consciousness and oblivion. He scarcely had time to consider his plight before Phrygia let loose with a mournful wail, a barbarous procession of moans and cries at once passionate and unrelenting. The rolling tide of an etheric sea washed over his body in icy waves. Lost within the rising current, his surroundings fell away from him.

A phantasmal tapestry of moving images unfolded before him as if in a dream, quickly coming to subsume his senses to the exclusion of all else. Concealed beneath the shadow of a precipice stood a long-forgotten house, a temple of automatism enwrapped in the embrace of a night that knew no end. Winding stairs reached down through the cellar, extending far beneath the surface of the earth. They plunged through richly decorated chambers and ornate stone cloisters, crypts and sanctuaries both lavish and austere, concealed tunnels that ran like rivers through living veins of stone, proceeding deep into the fiery heart of the subterranean world. An ivory throne arose in the vastness of the underground landscape that resided below. There, in the center of the inmost abode, sat the master of the house, his body stark and white as chalk while his face was yet concealed.

An undulating host of animals proceeded around the luminous throne: dogs and foxes, goats and wolves, a massive stag and several horses. Like an infernal carousel they danced and cavorted in a riotous display of obscene and vicious revelry. Some stood upright on their hind legs while others scampered on all fours. A rich cacophony of howls enveloped the base of the towering seat, threatening to rend the very ivory from which it was composed.

The bestial procession was overwhelmed by the unbearable presence of the monarch. His imperial essence surged and swelled like a potent electrical current, flowing back along innumerable routes to the interior of the house above. The force increased in volume, taking on the intensity of a deluge. It threatened to rip the lodgings from their foundations in the earth. Doors and windows burst their latches beneath the unrestrained and primal power while flames of blue and violet leapt from fundament to fingertip. The current lent its motive force to the sleeping machinations that were lodged within the walls of the now wracked and battered house. The stewards of the ancient temple rose up from their primal sleep, their jubilation issuing forth in an uncontrolled torrent of ecstasy and terror that resounded in waves throughout the soot-stained apparatus of the empire of night.

Albin couldn't bear a single second more. He lacked the constitution to sustain the vision. A further revelation lay in store for him, he knew, but it would simply have to wait. Wishing only to break away from the intolerable upsurge of unrestrained animal force, he disappeared through a covered arch that stood to one side of the marble engraving. He strode with brisk deliberation down an adjoining corridor as the bellowing voice of his host receded into the distance. He fled through a series of rooms and chambers, scampered down a narrow staircase, ducked without discrimination through a series of open doors. He'd had enough of the mysteries of the house for the time being and was eager to find his way back to the safety of the street.

He passed through a corridor submerged in thick darkness amidst distant creaks and mechanical groans. The throbbing churn of pistons reverberating from all sides menaced what was left of his nerves. He stepped from archway to antechamber, compelled to admit that he'd lost himself within the bowels of the mansion. It seemed entirely possible that the rooms and corridors were endless. A series of colored lights drifted by, bathing a row of hanging carpets in subtle hues of magenta and ochre. He imagined a control room hidden far below his feet from which invisible signals pulsed to every section of the house.

It occurred to Albin, as he quickly traversed yet another claustrophobic corridor, that it might have been wise to keep track of his orientation relative to his starting point. The carriage had rounded several winding curves and of course he'd paid no heed to the path he'd followed through the attics. He hadn't a clue as to which direction was most likely to lead him toward the ground floor. The interior of the house had proven to be much larger than he'd expected. Nevertheless, he remained steadfast in his conviction that if he simply wandered for long enough he'd find his way to an exit sooner or later.

At last he found a wide stairway which descended into a well-lit area. A crimson runner with gold and black flourishes partially covered the dark brown wood. The stairway opened out into a reasonable-looking sitting room with wooden chairs arranged among a pleasing display of coffee tables and bookshelves. Albin let himself drift down the stairs like a falling particle of dust, happy to be out of the attic and back among more agreeable surroundings. Here among the marble fireplace, the rich carpets, and the wooden panels, he felt that he'd returned to the part of the house that was intended for the public. He sat down in one of the chairs and allowed himself to rest, regaining his bearings after the turmoil into which he'd so unwittingly been thrust.

Leaning back against the rigid wood, he crossed one leg over the other in an attempt to derive some comfort from what was little more than a showpiece. He closed his eyes and let his head recline, allowing his tension to slowly drain away, yet not quite permitting himself to fall asleep. The clamor of machinery, still faintly audible, had receded to a safe enough distance. After an appreciable period of time had passed, he began to feel once again like a customer in an amusement park attraction.

He found himself again turning his thoughts to the painting he'd noticed on the back wall of the parlor.

For the first time since he'd seen it, he allowed himself to register the precise impact the image had exerted on him. Its details appeared with meticulous precision in his mind's eye. The barbarous chorus of contending winds, whipping the trees into an ecstasy of violence, seemed the expression of a power that could not be contained. The surrounding woods overflowed with this animal force. It transgressed the limits of reason. It clearly informed the inexplicable gaze of the tremendous mule that remained in the shadows. The man in the corner had looked so meek in contrast with the beast. He appeared completely passive in regard to his environment. It was as if he were a scrap of cloth caught in the fury of the storm. There was something exalted in the man's self-negation, an innocence that Albin found wholly desirable. This reinforced the notion that he could find refuge from what vexed him only by utterly renouncing his volition.

Ever since he'd left his childhood behind him, he'd secretly hoped that some sort of cataclysm would rush into his life and wash everything away. Though he'd scarcely allowed himself to think about it openly, there was a part of him that wished for nothing less than total oblivion. He longed to surrender to something so vast that he could scarcely comprehend it. Only thus might he realize the sovereignty that lay concealed in his shame.

He sat for a while longer, eyes closed and hands folded, his mind as vacant as a mirror in the dark. The perverse thought occurred to him that he might take up residency as a denizen of the house. He wondered if he might, in time, become a part of the mystery itself; whether the house would utterly consume him, absorbing him into its labyrinthine intrigues. Unable to determine whether this would be a positive development, he rose at last and set about the task of trying to find the exit.

Two tall, dark wooden doors, both closed, stood to either side of a Vienna wall clock which hung to one side of the stairway. A large archway dominated the opposing wall, while a far more modest opening provided egress near the fireplace. Albin was headed for the larger arch when he noticed that the rails in the floor didn't extend through the small doorway. They had extended down the stairs, they passed through the archway and beneath the two closed doors, and yet they ran right past the smaller opening without turning to cross over the threshold.

More curious than hopeful, Albin stepped through the opening, traversed a short, narrow corridor, and pulled the handle of the door in the far wall (unlocked, despite the quaint keyhole set into the brass plate). Passing through, he found himself in a cramped and darkened space, its walls only partially illuminated by the light from the sitting room. No more than a few paces before him could be seen the outline of an unshaded bulb. He ran his hand blindly over the wall beside him, searching for a switch. Within a couple of seconds, he'd found it and the room was bathed in a harsh, white glow.

It was clear that Albin had managed to find an altogether different section of the house. Walls of plain white drywall framed a room not much larger than a closet. The space was as plain as one could hope for. No attention whatsoever had been given to the décor. It was somewhat of a shock to emerge from the elegance of the house into such an unembellished environment as this. Even the attics had been filled with curiosities and antiques. Before him was a metal work table and a dismal little stool. The former was cluttered with tags and paint cans, iron files and tiny picks, unmarked plastic bottles, and paintbrushes of various sizes. An elegant hand of metal and plastic was propped up in one corner. A rusty shelf filled with similar artifacts hung on metal cables from the opposing wall. The austerity of the space evoked a feeling of deflation. There was no mystery here at all.

An unembellished doorway led to a darkened space beyond. Wondering if he'd have to feel his way through the dark, Albin proceeded through the tiny room, content that his adventure had come to an end. He was certain to find an exit soon, now that he'd left the attraction proper. A bank of fluorescent light panels flashed on overhead as he stepped into the hall. Motion detectors were clearly at work. The space was occupied by several rows of squat white racks, each one holding a selection of anatomy formed of painted plastic. A collection of naked torsos, frail parodies of the masculine ideal, stood lined up in a row before him. A line of brazen female frames began where the others left off. Arms, legs, waist-pieces, and heads were arranged in dizzying permutations along another wall. Albin recognized the scattered parts of each of the personas he'd encountered in the house and several more that were unfamiliar to him. The racks were staggered with tightly closed doors while an uninspiring doorway at the far end of the room lead further into darkness.

Albin passed from hall to hall beneath the glare of the fluorescent lights, his movements triggering the motion sensors as he entered each new area. He passed by a row of carriages lying nestled together on their sides. In another of the storage rooms, he encountered what looked like an old ticket booth fallen to mold and rot. Next to this stood several racks hung with suits and dresses sheathed in plastic bags. Albin wondered if the denizens of the house were given different clothes in different seasons, or if perhaps they changed their costumes in accordance with the phases of the moon. He found a stack of ringed binders inside an open cabinet on one of the walls. A brief examination revealed page after page of complex schematics and operating instructions. Agrippina, Phrygia, Tresler, and Klein each had a book of their own, while another, thicker volume contained details pertaining to the mechanics of the rooms themselves.

Unable to resist the pang of curiosity, he pulled down Agrippina's book and placed it on the surface of a nearby work table. A quick flip through the pages revealed circuit board diagrams and operating instructions, all of which were far too technical for him to comprehend. The latter sections of the book, while no less opaque, managed to capture his interest a little bit more. Mechanical blueprints were peppered with exotic-looking ciphers and charts of celestial influences.

One illustration in particular showed a series of hand gestures by which electrical impulses were made to flow through the limbs of the machine. Another diagram mapped the mirrors found throughout the house with the seasonal rotation of the stars. On another page, Agrippina was shown in an elegant pose before a full-length mirror. A beam of light from the reflection was split into seven colored fragments as it passed through the glass, the different colored rays anointing the mannequin's shoulders, wrists, brow, heart, and navel. Where the beam of light had come from, Albin didn't dare to guess.

He chanced upon a particularly unsettling image toward the back of the book. Agrippina was shown with naked bosom, her face a mask of icy disdain and her arms concealed in long gloves of black latex. She raised a sinuous leather whip high into the air above her head with the clear intent of unleashing its vengeance. Before and beneath her cowered a pitiable figure. He was shackled by several strands of rope to a tiny bamboo chair, his eyes bound by a silken blindfold and a rag stuffed in his mouth. The bearing of the figure bore the unquestionable mark of a broken and repentant man. Albin couldn't help but be affected by the merciless depiction. The cruelty of the automaton's demeanor was suffused into the very ink.

He closed the book without a trace of ceremony and placed it back upon the cabinet shelf. He nearly gave in to a desperate yearning to peruse Phrygia's binder as well, but he simply couldn't bring himself to take it into his hands. He somehow felt, despite the absurdity of the notion, that the act would be a violation of her trust. Perplexed, intrigued, and just a little dismayed with what he'd seen thus far, he continued onward in his search for an exit.

At last, encased within the darkness of a narrow corridor, he spied a dull red glow which beamed from a familiar panel of silver. The luminous exit sign dimly illuminated a heavy steel door below. A wave of sweet relief swept through his body. Salvation was at hand at last.

No piercing lights flashed overhead as he stepped into the corridor. The darkness was mostly undisturbed save for the luminous glow of the exit light. The opposing wall was taken up with an electronic display which spanned the entire length of the corridor. A moment's examination revealed a map of the house, complete with tracks and rails and flashing lights laid out with dizzying complexity. Each floor occupied a space of its own, while connecting links between the different levels were highlighted by colored lines. Albin was staggered by the byzantine arrangement.

He lost a couple minutes in an attempt to trace his path from room to room, first within the carriage and then on foot. So convoluted were the patterns in which the tracks branched and looped that his precise route was difficult to ascertain. Occasionally, a blinking light of orange or pale yellow would appear to move along one carriage rail or another, while flashing green lights danced from place to place along the rails set into the rooms themselves. Having located the library near the entrance to the ride, he traced a finger along a dark red line indicating the passage of the carriage to Klein's parlor. This much was easy, though he couldn't quite pinpoint the exact location at which he'd set off on his own.

The upper story of the house was truly vast, consisting of an open expanse partitioned by sliding walls, interior windows, narrow stairways, and claustrophobic passages. The space represented was large enough to contain several city blocks. The rails were arranged in intricate symmetries and codified motifs, their winding convolutions all converging upon a single, massive chamber. A title appeared above the latter in a flickering, electronic ghost-light: *The Chapel of the Ivory Sovereign*.

A glaring disc of brilliant white shone from within the tremendous vault, much larger than the flashing lights that appeared along the rails and in the other rooms. The shining beacon blazed with a furious intensity, pulsating slightly in the blackness and emitting fluctuating waves of incandescence. The far side of the chamber, behind the foreboding light, was left entirely open, as if to indicate a void.

Albin was not inclined to delay his exit further. He'd seen as much as he felt he needed to. He turned to leave, pushed the heavy door, which yielded with surprising ease, and was immediately faced with a steep and winding staircase. Down he went between the cold concrete walls. His descent was reasonably short and his surroundings unremarkable. Not so much as an iron rail accompanied the stone steps. Before he knew it, he faced another steel door. Upon passing through, he was confronted with the rain-soaked cobblestones of an ordinary city street beneath the starry night sky.

Eager as he was to make his departure, he paused before the exit. He reached a hand into the inner pocket of his overcoat. There he found the sovereign coin safely nestled between enveloping folds. He had no need to lay eyes upon it, he simply felt the urge to hold it for a moment between his fingers. He hadn't a clue where he might spend it or what he could procure with it. Perhaps, he thought, the purchase had already been arranged. He let the coin drop back into his pocket and proceeded onto the darkened street. The cool, night air embraced him without a trace of affection.

Cast out like an exile on unfamiliar shores, Albin felt distinctly naked as he left the building. Lost, perplexed, unsettled, and disoriented, he was no more certain of his place in the world than he was before he'd stepped into the carriage. That a veil had been pulled back was not in question. He'd borne witness to the ivory sovereign and it had changed something within him. He couldn't really say whether he'd found what he'd been looking for nor what direction his life might take as a result of what he'd seen. The city of his youth lay spread out before him as shameless and exposed as an intoxicated lover. He wished he could find refuge from the uncertainties that lay ahead, yet there was no place to retreat to, no sanctuary to abide in. With trepidation, he set out once more upon the desolate city streets, surrendering himself without reserve to the caprices of the night.

The Notary

THE Notary gave the customary signal for me to enter. I took my place on the green and gold upholstery of an empire-style armchair. I waited patiently as he attended to the needs of a client, a woman clad in an elegant dress of dark viridian. A single document lay on the wooden desk between them, its surface decorated with elegantly plotted curves, winding helixes, rhomboids delineated in intricate detail, and several passages in the manner of Euclid that had been hand-drafted in glistening ink.

"Your proofs are unassailable," said the Notary to his client. "And yet, a subtle inconsistency occasionally reveals itself within the vertex of an arc or along the line of intersection between two planes."

A pallor fell across the woman's face. It was evident that she was inconvenienced by his observation.

"Of course, the discrepancies will have to be accounted for," continued the impassive man. "Adjustments of this type are not entirely outside my jurisdiction. The document, unfortunately, cannot be notarized this evening, but arrangements can be made, official inquiries can be opened—I can see to it that the necessary modifications are applied within a reasonable amount of time."

"It would seem that I have little choice," spake the woman in a slightly acerbic tone.

"I'll send a messenger when the operation is complete," said the Notary before he sent the unfortunate woman on her way.

The house in which my friend offered his services was as commodious as ever. The most elaborate carpets concealed the sensuous resplendence of the polished floorboards. Polar maps and celestial atlases adorned the intricate shelves of several open armoires. The space was kept secure by a staff of painted matriarchs who kept watch over the premises from the confines of their gilded frames. The severity of their gazes exerted a slightly unsettling effect in combination with the angles of the furniture. At the back of the chamber hung an enormous painting of a midnight hunt. The procession advanced through the darkness of the winter woods as distant fires revealed the flanks of their immaculate, milk-white steeds. The faces of the riders themselves were obscured by helmets of alabaster.

Having purified his workspace with an offering of burning willow bark, the Notary poured me a glass of Armagnac. We sat across from one another before one of the expansive windows, the night sky outside gorged with radiant stars above a tangled conspiracy of elms and alders. We passed a pleasurable hour discussing the treason of the muses and the effect of their apotheosis on our respective trades. Our conversation turned, at length, to the woman seated at his desk when I'd arrived. "As chance would have it, your appearance could not be more propitious," he confided. "I wonder if you might afford me a minor courtesy."

What was needed, he explained, was a professional in my field of expertise to maintain the services of his office for a season. The correction of the document required an excursion into the forest that lay immediately outside the chateau. The trip would provide a considerable challenge for him. The woodland had a way of undermining all but the most persistent attempts at navigation. The office itself was nearly impossible to find. This, presumably, was the true reason for his client's discontent—she wasn't sure that she could manage to locate the Notary a second time. I myself had stumbled upon his chateau quite by accident, my intended destination having been a lecture at the Academy. My friend had set his hopes on setting out that very evening and was eager to attend to the necessary preparations. Happy to be of aid, I agreed to his proposal.

I waited patiently in my chair as he propitiated the matriarchs. Flaming bowls filled with aromatic herbs were set beneath their portraits, their iron surfaces engraved with supplications in the women's native tongues. A bottle filled with scarlet ink was upturned over an open atlas. The vibrant fluid soaked through several successive pages, each of them charting a region that bordered the Caucasus. The patterns formed between the ink and the defiled maps were then transcribed into a notebook. These were carefully converted into a series of coordinates according to a formula derived from ancient cartographers. When at last the Notary took his leave, I was left without instruction as to the minutiae of his trade. I understood that I was expected to proceed through intuition alone.

The elegance of the chateau was pleasantly suited to my tastes. I grew quite comfortable sitting behind the dark wooden work desk beneath the ample incandescence of the lamps. Spring was followed by the onset of winter—the seasons progressed backwards in the region in which the office was located. A regular succession of clients kept me busy, while my free time was spent sipping coffee and Armagnac beneath the relentless scrutiny of the women in their portraits. When the solstice approached and the Notary had not yet returned I grew increasingly concerned as to his welfare.

On the afternoon before the onset of the longest night, I was visited by a courier with a message from my friend. An egg was placed, with meticulous care, upright on one end upon the center of the work desk. Its upper section was circumscribed with but a single written line. "Need assistance," read the handwritten text, which had been penned in glistening ink. "Imperium descends by night at unwholesome latitudes." The messenger left without a word of explanation.

Casting my eyes around the office, I noted, with alarm, that the matriarchs had vanished from their portraits. In their places stood abandoned bell towers, desolate boudoirs, cloisters fallen into dismal solitude, and arches with their capstones lying shattered on the earth below. The view from the western windows confirmed that the last rays of the winter sun had begun to put themselves to sleep. So violent a sense of foreboding overtook me that I determined to go forth, unprepared, into the winter woods. I left the chateau at the onset of night, hardly troubling myself to consult a map and taking not so much as a lamp to light my way.

The alders embraced me like a foreign dignitary having come into their country on a diplomatic mission. Every courtesy was afforded me beneath the shadows of their branches. I was protected from the piercing wind, from the duplicity of reason, and from the precarious stratagems of the ecliptic. Even the stars were kept veiled, lest I fall prey to the fascinations that inspired sailors to cast themselves into the open sea. I was aware that a high honor had been bestowed upon me, by the grace of which alone was I permitted safe passage.

My perambulations took me to the opening of a mine shaft that reached deep into the dark heart of the earth. The wooden frame resided in a flickering pool of golden light, the flames that seethed to either side having burned without oil since the time before the first siege of Jerusalem. Fearful that my wandering would continue without end were I to forsake this propitious gift, I took up a torch and began my ill-prepared descent. The tunnel accepted me as if I were an offering, divesting me of my family name and of all the distinctions that had been bestowed upon me by my lineage.

In the upper levels of the mine, I came across a chamber strewn with heavy church bells, their alloys cracked and stained with age and blackened by the residue of sulfur. By the light of my torch, I discerned the names of Russian saints engraved onto their surfaces.

One in particular captured my attention, its perimeter inscribed with a flowing script displaying the requiems of Eudoxia of Moscow. Curiosity alone compelled me to take the rope by hand and pull it gently toward me. A wail of penitence emerged from the hollows of the bowl, sinking beneath the weight of its own haunting beauty and echoing like a descending dove down through the depths of the caverns below.

As I persisted ever further, passing from desolate ruin to diabolical splendor, I became increasingly aware of a tumult somewhere far above. The blast of long-horns and the rhythmic thud of horse's hooves shook the blackened walls of the claustrophobic caverns. In my mind's eye, I beheld the terror of the wild hunt—the banners of the horsemen strewn with viscera and set aflame, the procession of a company of idiot savants arrayed in archaic and unholy formations, high walls of ancient stone shattered and forsaken while the hordes pursued a fleeing victim whose martyrdom had seduced an empire. I couldn't help but wonder if it was the Notary himself that was hunted. As the clamor passed into the distance, I grew increasingly certain that they were closing in on the chateau.

Mastering my trepidation and continuing my descent, I emerged at last into an expansive and well-lit chamber. The matriarchs themselves awaited me there among pillars of carved ivory and bright limestone arches. White marble tiles were lit by flaming chandeliers that swung in arcs from a high, vaulted ceiling. The women stood mute and imperious before me, the shifting shadows passing over their bodies like the limbs of disconsolate spirits. Their faces were identical but for their expressions, each of which betrayed a principle that had been engraved into the soul of the world. Due to my time spent in the Notary's chateau, I had come somewhat to understand them. They perpetuated a bloodline without origin, and as such they were the administrators of an unspeakable authority.

Relinquishing my last remaining dignities, I passively put myself into their care. Having been stripped of everything by which I might be identified, I came dangerously close to receiving the sacrament of anonymity. I was hardly unaware of the impending possibility that the night might claim me as its own; nor was I inclined to deny the solstice its due.

The women solemnly took me into their arms and laid me in an open coffin. The box was filled halfway with ash and painted with the icons of Saint Nicetas of Novgorod and Abraham of Smolensk. My body was adorned with orchids and passed beneath the pungent fumes of hundreds of burning roots. Thus began a torchlit procession through the deeper levels of the mine. I was carried high above their heads as the torchlight traced ineffable mysteries on ancient walls of malachite. They sang funerary dirges as we descended, their wails and lamentations resounding through the torrid air like the hymns of telluric sirens. Thus did I pass the midnight hour of the solstice as the house whose care had been entrusted to me blazed like an abandoned pyre beneath the insolvency of winter stars.

My journey ended in a modest chamber located deep within the bowels of the rock. When I was lifted from the coffin, I was surprised to find myself confronted with none other than the Notary himself. The woman who had been his client stood beside him, the folds of her viridian dress shimmering in the torchlight. "There is one final service I will require of you," the Notary announced. "After this, you will be free to go." The couple, so it transpired, were to be married in that chamber, and I was to be the officiator. Once more, I readily agreed to help my friend. I considered it an honor, and, in any case, I had little choice. The marriage was performed, the vows exchanged, and the sacred bond secured in the eyes of the Holy One. On an altar before them lay the woman's document, signed and notarized at last.

The Hieromantic Mirror

IT is evening. I gaze with a distracted eye upon a row of tall arched windows at the far end of the dining hall. The occasional flash of lightning electrifies the flat black sky. We sit beneath a pleasant arrangement of hanging lamps and gilded tiles, protected from the raging elements on the other side of the glass. I would prefer to be outside in the pouring rain, to be subject to the relentless assault of the howling winds, the rich cacophony of thunder, the uncontrolled violence of nature, to be far removed from the oppressive gentility of the man who sits across from me.

Edgar is given to his usual suspicions. He accuses me of having 'fallen under questionable influences'. Dinner has been taken in a perfectly agonizing silence. The very way in which he wields his knife and fork comprises a calculated affront. He cannot stand the thought of control slipping through his fingers once again. At times like this, I rue the day I married him.

I would like to think that we have an agreement between us. A workable arrangement. We keep each other comfortable as long as it's convenient. I have my things.

He has his. We don't ask questions that we don't want answers to. In my typically logical fashion, I've made the same mistake I always do. I assume that people want what's best for them.

An irrational display of anger was unleashed in the hotel room before we came down to take our evening meal. As if in response, a veritable deluge has been let loose upon us. Raindrops pelt the windows like ejected rifle shells as lightning sets fire to the horizon. In a perfect world, a final crack of thunder would rend the heavens once and for all, splitting the sky asunder in a fiery conflagration. Our hopes, our fears, our dreams and aspirations would be returned to us anew, stripped of the lies with which we embellish them. If men like Edgar have any hope of touching the essential, he'll find it only in the heart of catharsis.

Silk napkins, hardly touched, lie naked on the stark white tablecloth, their folded forms like angels having fallen from the chandeliers. We abide in a fortress of opulent solitude among the other guests. We sit across from one another and say nothing, intent only on finishing our meal. Where Edgar's silence is contentious, mine is merely evasive. So long as I remain passive for long enough, he'll forget the indiscretions which he is certain I keep skillfully concealed from him.

I am guilty of every kind of infidelity, yet I've never shared a bed with another man or woman. I've been faithful to the letter, if not the spirit, of my marriage vows. I refuse to live entirely within the bounds of what is deemed acceptable. I am a woman given to particular inclinations. I don't expect them to be understood by those who would confine themselves to only one side of the mirror.

Now the dinner plates are taken from us. Now the dessert wine is poured into tiny crystal goblets. Edgar seems to have regained his composure for the time being. We make pleasant conversation amidst the occasional crack of thunder. He can be so delightful when he's not worked up. I let myself relax into the rich décor of the dining hall, the dignified arches above the doorways, the sumptuous curves etched into the tiles at our feet. The easy pleasure of being on vacation has returned to me at last. All the same, I remain braced for the next outburst.

Later, in our room, as Edgar sleeps, I position myself in a chair before the heavy wooden writing desk. If he wakes, I'll appear to peruse the pages of an open book on the desk before me, while in truth I'm engaged in a focused contemplation of the patterns in the wallpaper. Elaborate flourishes of ebony on cream damask stare back at me. The floral pattern etches itself into my retina, establishing its soft cartography in the subtle regions of my memory. I lose myself, through a prolonged abandonment of effort, within the intricate curves and arcs of the arrangement. Countless ports of entry reveal themselves among the endlessly repeated motifs. I wander through their permutations in the hope of locating a hidden passage—something which will take me to the courtyard that I so desperately seek.

Beyond the courtyard lies the Consulate, and in the Consulate awaits the Consul. I cannot hope to fully satiate my desire in this way. I must content myself with a brief encounter, a tête-à-tête and nothing more. A mere acknowledgement is all I hope for. It will suffice for now.

I pass through a succession of narrow passages, emerging from an alleyway into an open square. A rich mosaic of blackbirds chokes the open sky above the high white walls that rise to all sides. Yellow flowers wither on the vines that cling to shuttered windows and barred doors. Their fallen petals coat the tiles like pages torn from holy books. I step into an opening beneath a decorative arch. Tangled sheets of moss conceal a succession of doors without handles. I can't shake the feeling that I'm being pursued—by Edgar perhaps, or somebody else. The slight tinge of paranoia serves only to exalt the flame of my desire.

At last, I slip through a tall gate and onto the Consulate grounds. A stone fountain rises from an octagonal pool before a magnificent façade crowded with dark windows and ivory columns. A wide stairway rises to one side, flanked by stone sphinxes on granite pedestals. At the summit of the stairway stands the tall imposing doors that lead to the Consulate's Library.

One of the side-doors of the main building swings open. An official emerges. He carries a copper tray upon the upraised palm of one hand. The winds pick up, gently ruffling the ivy which clings to the manor walls. The official stops before me. A rectangular box of dark, unpolished wood stands upright upon the surface of the tray. The hinged lid is open, and a stack of stiff paper cards rises from its inner chamber. I select a card from the middle of the deck. On it is pictured a red-crowned crane, a bird cherished by the Japanese for its rarity. Elegant patches of black and white enwrap its body like calligraphy. The card's reverse is as desolate as a field of freshly fallen snow.

The official has withdrawn. I turn my attention from the card to the manor before me. The stars emerge like jeweled daggers in a sky of incandescent liquid. In one of the high windows, illuminated from behind by a tawny glow, stands the silhouette of the Consul. I can sense his overwhelming majesty, though his face is veiled by the contrast of light and shadow. All the same, his gaze penetrates the sanctity of my heart. I relish the flair of violent passion which his distant presence arouses within me. It is for this sensation that I've come here. With one finger I stroke the surface of the card, tracing delicate circles around the image of the crane. The rare bird is our point of contact in this place. Its exotic hues transmit a steady signal from my fingertips to the icy surface of the window, to the shadow cast upon the heavy wooden frame, and to the light that radiates beyond.

A firm hand upon my shoulder extracts me from the intimacy of our engagement. I return to myself, fully present in the hotel room. Edgar stands behind me, having not uttered a single word. He doesn't have to. I can feel the severity in his touch. I manage to collect myself a little before addressing him. "I must have drifted off," I say as I look down at my book. "One too many glasses of dessert wine for Mrs. Chamberlain."

"The Moscato did a number on me as well," he says. His voice, though softer than his touch, is anything but sleep-affected. He's probably been watching me for quite some time now. "I don't think it's meant to be consumed in such large quantities," he continues. "Once we got started, of course, it was hard to stop." He lifts his hand from my shoulder and returns to the bed, seating himself on one side. "Anyway, I thought you might prefer to spend the night in bed with your husband, rather than sitting in your chair and gazing wistfully at the wallpaper."

"Of course," I softly mutter. Just to torment him, I take an eternity to disrobe.

Edgar is not a cruel man, nor is he intolerant or dispassionate. He is not even especially jealous. He would like to think that I'm merely an eccentric, given to such naive diversions as crystal gazing and spiritism. I've told him, truthfully, that I have no interest in such banal devices. These are things he could abide by, things he could put a name to. What he cannot accept is anything that lies entirely outside of his understanding. There is an inseparable rift between us, yet it's his very conventionality that I so cherish. It's imperative that I remain rooted in his world, at least in part. The rarefied milieu of the Consul exerts a dangerous fascination upon me. I could easily succumb to it as if it were a drug, becoming more and more dissociated from worldly affairs. Edgar keeps me firmly tethered to matters of practical interest. I've come to depend upon the worst aspects of his personality.

*

I stand on the balcony outside of our room as the late

afternoon wind caresses my skin. The storm has abated. The sun has returned. The charming little town unfolds before me with its winding alleys, narrow stairways, and tall windows. A white cat makes its way from one stone ledge to another, its tail twitching like a dowsing stick as it extends a cautious paw across the gap. I watch it disappear between the iron rails of a gate, its ivory feet gingerly skipping over the dark tiles beyond.

Edgar has been tense all morning. Tomorrow, we return home. I let my impatience burn within me like an exquisite flame. Very soon, I will again meet with the Consul face-to-face. My confinement to the courtyard has made the prospect of returning all the more compelling.

A short while afterward, I manage to sneak another excursion to the manor grounds. I've found a place of sanctuary at the bottom of a stairway not far from the hotel. It's a forgotten place, concealed by its unremarkable simplicity—cramped, slight, and uninviting. A modest fountain is attached to one wall. The mouth of a lion rendered artlessly in time-worn stone spits a steady stream of water into the shallow basin. The miniscule space is entirely enwrapped in a veil of soft blue shadow.

Sitting upon a stair, still damp from last night's rain, I allow myself to drift into a pleasurable torpor. The continual sound of water splashing in the fountain echoes throughout the intimate enclosure. I lean back against a wall of stone, allowing the coolness of the concrete beneath my palms to recede into the distance. Fleeting phantoms of masonry and brickwork surge forth and disperse before my inner eye—finely carved stone pillars, a wrought iron trellis covered in ivy, a stairway descending deep into the heart of the earth. I maintain a trace of lucidity, like a single sentry posted before the mouth of an abyss—a flame of wakefulness which flickers in an ocean of oblivion. My lamp is meager, but it is enough for me to plot a course through the hypnagogic labyrinth while my body sleeps.

It isn't difficult to find the courtyard. By the time I pass through the familiar gate, I'm in full possession of the finer of my faculties. I occupy a body woven of the light of memory and sustained by little more than desire. Within this vehicle I move through a world that lies concealed behind the mirror of the senses.

It is dark. A rolling tide of black cloud has swallowed up the sky above me. The dim light shining from an upper window just barely illuminates the fountain, the surrounding tiles, and the imperious columns before the entrance to the manor. Again, the Consul awaits me in the window. I can clearly see his face this time. His presence, on the other hand, seems hollow and withdrawn. He stands immobile, a statue, an empty shell. His gaze is fixed upon the surface of the glass rather than on what lies beyond it. Might his restraint be taken as an invitation to transgress my limitations, to cross the delicate boundary imposed by the nature of my means of travel? Or might he himself be traveling, making use of the play of light and shadow on the surface of the window in the same way that I myself have done with the patterns in the wallpaper, the elaborate formations on the carpet in the hotel lobby, the tapestries of moss and ivy upon the walls of the surrounding buildings?

A drop of rain strikes my cheek like a pinprick of gentle light. Just as I begin to wonder if the sensation was imagined, another strikes my wrist. The shadows grow darker as the winds pick up. A flash of lightning illuminates the courtyard for a fraction of a second followed by complete darkness. A moment later the sky unleashes a veritable torrent upon me. The distant roll of thunder accompanies the frenzied sound of rain-drops striking the tiles. The chill of the phantasmal waters saturates my subtle body. The light cast by the high window is far dimmer now, its radiance fails before it reaches the pillars below. The Consul no longer appears behind the glass.

I remember my wish from the night before to immerse myself in the wrath of nature. I yield to the downpour, resisting nothing of its force, submitting myself to the severity of elements no less visceral for their insubstantiality. A second flash of thunder alights the courtyard. This time I happen to be facing the Library. One of the stone sphinxes, illuminated by the flash, has risen to its hind legs, its front legs raised into the air as if to attack some unseen assailant. In the roar of thunder that follows I can dimly hear the sound of hooves beating against the ground in a ferocious panic. A tumultuous collision can be heard in the direction of the manor. The sound of rain striking the tiles becomes a stampede, drowning out all else. The calamity threatens to consume the vision. I can no longer sense the ground beneath my feet. A final crack of lightning illuminates a frightful scene—a blackbird rising from a nest of tangled serpents.

My visit to the Consulate has ended. I've returned to the unyielding stone of the stairway near the hotel. Heavy rain, as real as my nearly soaked-through dress, pours down in unrelenting torrents. I am freezing cold and thoroughly drenched.

I rush up the stairs, intent on returning to the hotel and taking a hot bath. Edgar awaits me at the top of one of the stairways. He's dressed appropriately for the weather in a heavy black coat and hat. He holds his trench coat open for me, his smiling face a beacon of warmth and delight. His glasses make him look like a professor or an over-zealous legal assistant. I rush into his embrace. He wraps his coat around my shivering shoulders. He smells of wet wool, aftershave, and kindness. I press my body against his, glad to be in his company. He is an angel of earthly delights and I adore him for it.

✦

Late evening at home. Edgar studies maps of Dante beneath the soft glow of a hanging lamp while I sip yellow Chartreuse and gaze through one of the windows at the pouring rain. The occasional tantrum blazes across the sky, casting arcane shadows on the bookshelves and the liquor cabinets, beautifully illuminating the wind-swept poplars on the other side of the lake.

The shelves are stocked with nearly as many wooden boxes as they are with books. They contain elaborate maps of mathematical landscapes, carved idols, cubes and pyramids—all marked up with icons and symbols at once simplistic and arcane. Most of these items are old and very rare. My husband is a collector. He enjoys playing the games he collects in the evenings and I am more than happy to indulge his passion. Occasionally, I pilfer a piece from one set or another to take with me to the Consulate. Edgar is furious when he comes across a game with a missing piece, all the more so for the fact that, while he knows that I have stolen from him, he cannot for the life of him fathom why.

His fascination with maps, with symmetry, and with carefully balanced rules remains distinct from my own interest in these areas. Where he is an academic, I am a sensualist. While he plays his games to study, I play to win. His inclination is toward the abstract, yet he's bound to the world of the intellect. What I pursue is more tenuous still and I'm free to live in any world I choose to. I can hardly deny the rarified pleasure that comes from living the life of the mind, yet I could never satisfy myself with such a life. I am a woman possessed of insatiable desires and am ever compelled to push beyond my limitations. The flames of ancient torches beckon to me from beyond the veil of the reasonable world.

"You're working at the Consulate tomorrow, I presume?" His head remains buried in his studies. My face is toward the window, I can't see him, but he is a man of habit and I know his habits well.

"I work my usual shift," I reply as I peer at the lake through my glass of Chartreuse. The flash of distant lightning, tinged bright yellow through the liqueur, takes on the appearance of a burst of sunlight upon the face of the water.

"It's just as well," he says, the soft roar of thunder nearly drowning out his naturally quiet voice. "I'll be buried in my work all day."

"And what does Mr. Chamberlain work on these days?"

He looks up. I can feel his gaze upon the back of my neck. "Mr. Chamberlain," he says, "is working on an article. The first in a series, if all goes well, of an extended commentary on the *Libro de los Juegos* of King Alfonso the Tenth. I expect it to be nothing less than groundbreaking."

"And where does Mr. Chamberlain plan to publish his study?"

"Mr. Chamberlain has not a single hopeful prospect," he laments. "He's been cast out of the kingdom and his bridges have been thoroughly burned. He is bereft, forlorn, and utterly destitute. Yet still he forages onward, having a noble and courageous heart."

"Well, I think Mr. Chamberlain is very admirable." I turn around at last. "And furthermore, I would very much like to read his work when he's finished with it."

"I'll see what I can do, Mrs. Chamberlain." His gaze is tempered with levity. "I think I can arrange it, though I can't promise you exclusivity."

"I should hope not, Mr. Chamberlain," I say, the cleansing sting of the Chartreuse in my mouth. "I should indeed hope not."

Black coffee in the early morning before the drive out to the Consulate. It's cold. The morning mist has yet to clear. Once I'm off the main road the streets are nearly empty. I exult in the fog-bound landscape. I push my vehicle beyond any semblance of a reasonable speed. Driving alone in the early morning is pure pleasure, power, mystery. Remote and winding mountain roads. Grey sky with a tinge of violet. Black driving gloves. I could easily remain behind the wheel until the sun goes down again.

For all of my reckless impulses, I take the necessary precautions. A woman in my position must not be heedless. I have responsibilities which I take very seriously. I swiftly make my way up the winding road that leads to the Consulate. By the time I arrive the mist is just beginning to clear.

I notice, as I leave my vehicle, that one of the sphinxes before the Library has been damaged. A minor, yet noticeable, crack appears in one of its front legs. As I approach the entrance to the manor, I note also that one of the pillars has been gouged. I pass through the front door and into a lobby encased in smooth white marble. From there, I proceed up an ivory stairway and past the surrounding balustrade. Small statues rise from the elegant rail. Their lithe black bodies hold tall yellow bulbs that taper like ascending flames. Their ceramic faces scrutinize me as I pass by them. The upper reaches of the Consulate are especially well guarded. I pass through a corridor beneath a high arched ceiling. At last I stop before a pair of doors with polished, golden handles. A plaque affixed to the wall to one side identifies the room beyond. I pass through the doors and into *The Chancel*.

I'm greeted by three men that sit at the far end of a long table. Before them lies a wooden board and several hand-carved game pieces. The air is heavy with tension and anticipation. The game is *Xiangqi*, a development of the Indian game *Chaturanga*. The pieces, small discs of red agate, are arranged among the intersecting points of a grid: two opposing Emperors and their advisors, along with elephants, canons, rooks, chariots, and foot soldiers. The board is divided by a horizontal passage representing the Yellow River, the winding serpent that irrigates the heart of China. At the head of the table sits the Consul. His manner of dress, like my own, is appropriate to his office. He is restrained and professional, outwardly calm, his dignity unblemished and his politesse impeccable. He appears to be no different than any other man, yet I have beheld his mysteries unveiled, I have tasted of his unseen virtues, I have courted the intrigues of the secret fire that courses through his blood. He is not at all the man that he appears to be. If he were, he could not fulfill his role here at the Consulate.

For the moment, he presents nothing more than the face of a perplexed official. His gaze is concentrated on the board and the arrangement of the pieces. "It's a good thing you've come," he says at last, looking up from the uneven distribution of agate on the game board. "We're faced with a little bit of a situation, as you can see."

I seat myself upon the edge of the table, one palm planted face down before the game board. The other men lean back a little in their chairs, happy to relinquish their responsibilities, though the tension of the game still grips them. They're not strangers to me. I've worked with them on other occasions—sometimes closely, sometimes at a distance.

I sit in a concentrated study of the board. I let my gaze blur. The pattern made from the various pieces congeals into an icon. I allow the familiar process to work through me. It's not a matter of strategy as much as it's a process of remembering, though I can hardly say from whence the memory comes. I place a finger upon the surface of one of the pieces, an elephant stationed on the near side of the river. The sensation of the piece beneath my fingertip recalls impressions long since lost to me: half-forgotten myths of childhood, emotions at once nostalgic and perplexing, a subtle certainty which taints the blood that courses through my ancestry. I assemble my familiar spirits with necromantic precision. I let them wash over me, welcoming them into the landscape of my body. I seek a level of intimacy with the piece—with its physicality, its history, its unspoken associations. There is a type of truth that can be known through touch alone. With very little thought, I push my piece across the river and onto a space on the other side. It is an illegal move, one that none of the assembled men, including the Consul, could have made. Not being officially employed at the Consulate, I am afforded certain liberties. After a moment's further consideration, I lift my finger and lean back, satisfied with my decision.

The release of tension in the room is tangible. The Consul recognizes at once that the problem has been solved. The others, sensing his relief, let themselves relax as well. One of the aides mops his brow with a silken handkerchief. "It's been a trying morning," says the Consul. "The violent weather has had its way with the electricity these last few days. Now this. What's more, vandals would seem to have done their work on some of the statuary on the grounds. Repairs are underway."

I need say nothing. The crisis has been averted. The men assembled in the room depart to their official habitations. I'm to meet with the Consul in *The Sacristy* in a quarter of an hour. I walk over to one of the windows and peer out between the red velvet curtains. The Consulate is located on a small plateau which juts out from the slope of a fairly impressive hill. A wooded landscape rises to the north behind the manor. Through the window, I can just make out the last traces of the morning mist which swallows the upper branches of the trees that approach the peak.

I turn back to the *Xiangqi* board. My game piece resides in conspicuous defiance against the Huang He, the river that divides one side from the other. I imagine its waters overflowing, swelling beyond their established boundaries, drowning the pieces that lie in their immediate proximity. The waters are at once regenerative and poisonous. The winding serpent has been known to turn and strike, injecting its deadly venom into the dark earth to the peril of all who walk upon it. By making an illegal move against the river, I've defied its treachery. There will be consequences. I leave the pieces as they stand and head to the *The Sacristy*.

The Consul is there waiting for me. Red painted walls with dark trim contain a cozy, yet efficient office. Black lacquer frames border monochrome portraits of mythological landscapes and impossible feats of architecture. Cabinets of wicker and dark wood are stocked with exquisitely carved stone idols and iron bowls for burning incense. I join the Consul on a dark divan that resides next to a heavy crimson curtain flanked by silken ropes of gold. Steam rises in luxuriant folds from a white teacup on a low table before him. Before we speak, I remove a game piece of my own from my small gray leather clutch—a cylinder of ivory in the vague form of a tower. It was taken from Edgar's collection. It is an uncommon piece, belonging to a German *Asalto* board from the second half of the eighteenth century. The game is a variant of *Fox and Geese*. Edgar won't be happy when he finds it missing. One must act according to one's higher interests. I press the piece with gentle insistence into the Consul's palm.

He examines the object closely, impressed by its fine character. "It's certainly a piece of remarkable distinction," he says, turning it over with the fingers of one hand. He rises, walks over to a low wooden table, where I join him. The surface of the table is inset with a detailed map of Europe. After a moment's thought, he places the piece on the border between two countries. An adequate choice.

"I must admit to more than a little concern regarding the trouble we had outside the Library the other night." He returns to the divan, sits, and places one hand upon his knee. "I'm sure you're aware that it wasn't vandals that caused the problem with the statuary outside."

"You worry overmuch," I tell him. "The Library is unassailable. Even if someone were to find a way in, they'd scarcely know what to do once they got there. Our archives are inscrutable to anybody not in possession of the proper keys."

"We must be careful nonetheless," he says. "If only for the sake of appearance. There are very specific procedures that must be carried out in the case of a breach, protocols that must be followed to the letter. There's always a little bit of danger involved. These things are not easy by any means. It's essential that we don't allow the natural balance to be upset." His gaze rises to meet mine. "I assume that you're aware how important your position is to the sanctity of our operations? If such a thing were to become necessary, that is."

I join him. We sit in silence, each on our own side of the divan, he with spine held rigid and with his teacup in one hand, me with one elbow settled on the armrest, hands folded before me and one leg over the other. As he sips his tea, I let my gaze rest on the intersection between two panels on the lower wall. There is a place within the heart in which the holy and the bestial embrace. This place lies far beneath the sediment that supports the baser emotions. It is precisely in this place that the god within exercises its dominion. This is the level on which we interact—unseen, unheard, unsuspected. This is the level on which our innermost desires are transmuted into civil service.

We converse, though it hardly matters what we say. An official brings the day's requests. There are visas to process, export transactions to review, minor issues that require special attention. There is also a document from the Embassy. The latter lies outside of my field of expertise, nor do I have the clearance necessary to receive communications from our parent institution. I must leave these matters to the Consul. The requests are sorted and we head each to our respective offices. After a couple of hours, we meet again in *The Sacristy*. The Consul takes his tea with a splash of brandy.

"Tell me about the Embassy," I say—a polite request as I lean back on the divan.

He is reticent, as is to be expected. "We do not speak openly about the Embassy here at the Consulate."

"Then speak furtively," I tease. "I would have you regale me with tales of your exploits with the Ambassador."

"I couldn't tell you even if I wanted to," he says in a voice of gentle admonition. "I've never once laid eyes on the Ambassador."

"Tell me lies, then."

"Even to lie about the Ambassador is to say too much," he says. "I hardly wish to profane the sacred."

He looks so imperious with his dark jacket and silver cuff links. His façade is perfect. His manner projects a flawless image of the serious civil servant, yet in truth he is an auger, oracle, and priest, and I am at once his acolyte and adversary. The secrets that he keeps reveal more than anything that he could possibly tell me. I harbor guilty thoughts. In my hermetically sealed heart I find myself wishing for a catastrophe. An assault upon the Library would open up such fascinating doors. I can't help but yearn to pass beyond the boundaries imposed upon me. To deny this aspect of my nature would constitute a type of sacrilege. The Consul senses the germ of corruption that flames within my heart. He is powerless to disapprove—he depends upon it every bit as much as I do.

Early evening at home. I sip an after-dinner cocktail with my husband over a game of *Nine Man's Morris*. The game is not an official part of his collection. It's a recent set. The board and pieces have been manufactured by a machine. The containing box, made of cardboard, is printed with modern designs. It's of interest to him only as a means of enjoyment when he needs to tear himself away from his more serious work.

Edgar makes a move in haste. A poor choice, though I suspect that he's orchestrating an elaborate setup in order to entrap me. "What kinds of things do you get up to while you're...at the Consulate?" He appears to be engaged in a focused study of the board.

"I do precisely what's required of me," I respond. "Nothing more." It's not the first time that he's asked this question.

"And that is...?" he probes, looking up from the board.

"I'm afraid that's classified information."

"Why can't you just talk to me about it?" He's almost pleading now. It's positively embarrassing. He looks up at me without a trace of dignity. It's unbecoming of the man I'd like for him to be.

"I can," I say with eyes averted. "I simply choose not to." I move a piece from one square to another.

"You infuriate me, Mrs. Chamberlain," he says as he puts into effect his would-be coup de grâce, an admittedly devastating and unexpected move.

"I do my best, Mr. Chamberlain," I respond, picking up his piece and gently tossing it into the fireplace. Unfortunately, the fireplace has not been lit. The piece falls with a dull thud into a shallow pile of ash.

He draws in his breath, picks up one of my pieces, leans back on the couch, and drops it without a trace of ceremony into the fish tank, where it swiftly sinks to the bottom. I'm relieved to see at least a hint of the man I married.

I, in turn, toss another of his pieces out the window. The frame is open just a crack. The piece barely makes it through.

Edgar leans forward and, with droll eyes fixed upon my own, upsets the board. The pieces tumble like the bodies of fallen soldiers at my feet. "I've never been so insulted in my life, Mr. Chamberlain," I say. "I must insist that you make love to me in order to atone for your atrocious behavior."

"I'll see what I can do, Mrs. Chamberlain," he leans back on the couch. "I think I can arrange it, though I can't promise you exclusivity."

I almost wish he wasn't joking.

+

Hours have passed. Edgar is furiously scribbling in his notebook at the writing desk. His typical response to an amorous encounter is to make up for lost time by retreating into his intellectual pursuits. There seems to be a direct connection between his libido and his head.

"The ancients sought to reduce the complexity of the world to a simple set of rules applied to a basic structure," he announces as he closes his notebook with one hand. "The game board is an oracle, a mirror of the soul. The true object of play is to come to understand the secret laws by which all things arise and pass."

As usual, he has a rudimentary grasp of theory, yet he misses all of the finer points of practice. It would never occur to him to seize control of his own destiny. He's rendered impotent by his inability to pass beyond his intellect. The mysteries he so desperately seeks are visceral, not intellectual. Mastery has as much to do with the body as it does with the mind. To truly understand, one must be willing to transgress. Edgar is too delicate to take the necessary steps. They must be taken unprompted, with no instruction. He simply doesn't have it in him. There are sacrifices involved. If you wish to penetrate the veil, you must allow yourself to first be broken. I'd been crushed, ground to fine powder, incinerated and had my ashes scattered before ever I attained the first watchword of the outermost gate.

Still, he serves a purpose. Never thinking to set foot inside the temple, he contents himself with taking measurements of the front porch. His work will occasionally turn up something of interest. We need our scholars, after all. Edgar's greatest flaw is that he wishes to possess the very things that he can scarcely comprehend. There will always exist a tension between us, he will always bear resentment toward me. Not only have I learned to live with this, I've come to love him for it.

Edgar sips whiskey mixed with water. I drink a red Bordeaux. I feel nervous, slightly restless. A high-pitched buzzing arises as if in the distance, felt as much as heard. I become aware of a distinct metallic taste on the roof of my mouth. Something is happening. I can feel it. I suspect an attempt to breach the Library.

I tilt my wine glass nearly horizontal. The wine pools up on one side. As I begin to carefully rotate the glass, the lights from the hanging chandelier above me give rise to swirling streaks of luminescence on the shimmering surface of the liquid. The resulting pattern is intoxicating and perplexing—a fluctuating series of criss-crossing arcs that arise and dissolve as I turn the bowl. Several times I see the outline of the Consulate, the stairs before the Library, or the faintest suggestion of a standing sphinx, yet the images never coalesce enough for me to enter into them. There is interference. I can sense the presence of the Consul blocking my efforts. I assume that he's taking measures to protect the grounds, and that whatever it is that he's doing is serving to keep me away as well. Giving up, I finish the last swallow and go to bed.

Early the next morning, I speed along the winding roads at a nearly reckless pace. I'm eager to reach the Consulate, desperate to confirm the hint of trouble that I felt with such certainty the night before. Nature howls like a wounded animal beneath a sky of murky gloom as the wheels of my vehicle grip concrete still wet with last night's rain. Rays of icy sunlight shine like knives through breaks in the clouds above. If I could strike them with enough momentum, I might shatter them.

Upon arrival, I notice no visible signs of further damage. The sphinxes gaze with benign indifference across the muddy grounds, secure in their immobility. The fountain gushes forth in the crisp autumn air, its pure clear water splashing in the octagonal basin. I proceed to *The Chancel*, where I find two senior officials engaged in a game of *Sunjang Baduk*. The game board is carved onto the top of a tall box of black stained wood. The sides of the box are adorned with painted figures in white robes assembled around a copse of pale poplar trunks. I'd seen the elegant set and pieces only once before, shortly after an international incident had caused some trouble at the Embassy. I'm assured that the current game has been undertaken in order to address a comparatively minor matter. I am not afforded the pleasure of watching the strategies unfold. My presence has been requested, so I'm informed, in one of the upper floor offices.

Rarely am I summoned to the upper floors of the Consulate. They're typically reserved for operations of an especially delicate nature. I feel a definite change in atmosphere as I ascend the curving stairway into the dim light of the upper hall. A row of low-hanging chandeliers casts serpentine shadows onto the dark red carpets at my feet. The pale glow of their faded bulbs tints the ivory walls with a wash of saffron, abandoning the balconies above to languish in darkness behind their curving iron rails. I make my way to a narrow black door with no identifying title. I slip inside to find the Consul awaiting me alone.

The tiny office is cramped, austere, and windowless. The flames of tall white candles provide the only source of light. An understated carpet conceals the better part of a dark, wooden floor. Two unadorned chairs have been placed before a table. The Consul sits in one of them, his attention wholly focused on the objects before him. He glances up at me as I take my place in the empty chair that remains. "The Library has officially been breached," he tells me, his expression as impassive as ever. I know better than to press for further details.

The table is crowded with an assortment of objects: Chinese playing cards, a pair of dice, and a small selection of electronic devices, among other things. A book lies open to the Consul's left. I recognize the scarlet covers just visible beneath the smooth white pages. The book is the latest in a vast collection of meticulously compiled logs, a repository in which the outcomes of the most recent games are recorded. The upper section of one page is filled with characters in a script unknown to me. A dark brush, long and slender, rests against a bottle of black ink beside the book.

The hypnotic dance of candlelight is reflected in a dark green circle of convex glass set into a mechanical device that sits before three upturned cards. Beneath the glass is a rectangular speaker above a row of tiny dials. The Consul adjusts one of the dials with a cautious hand, turning it just a little at a time between long pauses. A stochastic hiss of static emerges from the speaker, barely audible. The cards are very old. They're tall and thin and covered with inscrutable designs in red and black. This is not the first time I've encountered them. They're taken from an eighteenth-century deck known to Chinese antiquity as *The Six Tigers*. The deck consists of thirty cards: three suits of nine and three additional members. Before me on the table lie the Three of Coins, the One of Strings, and the Three of Mariads—a basic query pattern used for communications with the Embassy.

The dice, bone-white with uneven black dots, sit in a triangle which has been etched directly into the surface of the table. To one side of the triangle is a sheet of paper, perfectly square, featuring a grid printed in lines of red ink. Chinese characters, hand-painted in rich black, appear in all but three of the squares. "The frequency shifts with the passing of time, the rolling of the dice, and the severity of the message," says the Consul, his eyes glued to the device before him. "I had them just a minute ago," he looks up at me. "We've been in session for the better part of the morning."

Communication with the Embassy is always difficult. They are rarely straightforward in their transmissions. They have particular protocols by which we must abide. They see things differently than we do. Their officials make use of paradox and contradiction. They see hidden harmonies where we see only conflict. We play our games according to their dictates, though at best we receive our orders only in the half-light. In the Embassy resides the book of strategies with which we strive to conform. Our own books, logs, and games are managed so as to deviate as little as possible from their mandates, or what we can derive from their mandates. Theirs is the template, ours the operative. Their book reveals the patterns, ours maintain the changes. They are the delegates of heaven, we are the executives of earth. Their vision of harmony is mysterious to us—the hidden order which we strive to embody lies always just beyond our grasp.

The Consul sighs. He takes his hand away from the dial. "I give up," he says, exasperated. "Feel free to give it a go if you'd like." He indicates the dice. His invitation takes me by surprise. Technically, I'm not even supposed to be here. I have no clearance for operations of this type. A definite line is being crossed. The Consul knows as well as I do that there will be consequences.

There is a further consideration. Clearly, my illegal move on the *Xiangqi* board had been anticipated. It is precisely this that has allowed the Library's defences to be circumvented. Can I be trusted with the dice? A misthrow might open up the possibility of communication from an entity other than the Embassy. We have no certain way of knowing precisely from whom it is that we receive our orders. The science of diplomacy is not exact. We're forced to proceed by chance and intuition.

Having accepted the possibility of error, I sit down and take the dice into my hands, steeling myself for the roll. I relish their weight in the bowl of my palm, luxuriating in the texture of the polished ivory against my fingertips. I regulate the flow of my breath and surrender to the providence of fate. It is an act of prayer, a ceremonial observance, the utterance of a sacred oracle.

With a clear mind and an open heart, I gently toss the dice back into the triangle. Their upturned faces display a six and a two.

The Consul adjusts the dials with care, searching for the closest viable frequency within the range indicated by the dice. There's a break in the static, followed by a rapid series of staccato bursts. I can nearly hear the roll and surge of ocean waves beneath the fuzz emitted by the speaker. I imagine a sky of indigo above them, the soft blue light of ancient stars gushing in the pulsating void. There's a noticeable shift in the atmosphere of the room. The flames of the candles flicker and swell. The Consul sits immobile, eyes glued to the device before him. The screen remains blank, empty, void. Within the soft deluge of noise can be heard a woman's voice, barely audible. She repeats a single word, in two-second intervals, speaking with an unidentifiable accent. Her diction is as articulate as it is without emotion. It takes a number of repetitions before I can discern the word she utters over and over again as if on a pre-recorded tape loop: *Cygnus... Cygnus... Cygnus...*

The Consul quickly scrawls two characters onto the open page of the book with the brush, one for the results of the dice roll and another for the response. The equipment is turned off, the brushes put away, the cards returned to their package. I know enough about our protocols to discern what must come next. Without a word, we proceed to *The Sacristy*.

Together we move the divan to one side of the spacious red room. We part the crimson curtains which conceal the far wall just enough to expose the marble altar that stands behind them. Nine shelves of dark, stained wood line the wall behind the altar. Short white candles on unadorned saucers form nine distinct columns on top of them. Brass bowls filled with white sand are placed on the far ends of the marble. Small discs of charcoal are carefully lit and placed in the sand. The Consul fetches two glass dishes, one containing stones of mastic, the other filled with galbanum. A phial of anointing oil and a silver bell are retrieved as well. I wait while the Consul lights the candles on the back wall, one for each of the stars in the constellation of the swan. The star formation is known as Tiān é Zuò, or Cygnus. The flaming lights suffuse the altar in a vibrant, heavenly glow, gently illuminating the dark wood shelves and the flat black wall behind them.

Moving the gaming table is somewhat of a ritual in itself. It is a plain white table, rising roughly to the level of my chest. At the time that the game commences, due to my position, it will reside just below my knees. During play I will sit while the Consul stands. The game with which we will engage the hands of destiny is called *Pai Gow*, easily among the oldest and most distinguished of the classic Chinese domino games. The dominoes themselves are exquisite works of art. Several hundreds of years old and hand-carved from bone, each one of them is longer than the span of my hand. They're arranged in two discrete stacks upon the table.

I take my place on the altar, the heat from the candles gently warming my back. The incense is ignited; a pinch of mastic to my right and a pinch of galbanum to my left. My sleeves are rolled up past the elbows, my skirt lifted to above the level of the knee. The bottom two buttons of my blouse are carefully unbuttoned by firm, yet respectful hands. I'm anointed with the holy oil in nine distinct places: on my brow, on the base of my neck, on my inner elbows and on one wrist, on my ring finger, my navel, and finally on each knee. The oil burns just slightly, enough to mark the sensation. The Consul places his lips on each of the nine points of my body in accordance with the ancient precept. He softly mutters a secret name for each of them, an invocatory formula designed to call forth the hidden genius of the presiding stellar deity. His warm breath suffuses the oil with his vital essence.

At last everything is prepared. The Consul takes his place on the other side of the table and surrenders himself to the hidden god which flames eternally within his breast. We lock eyes with one another, he rings the bell, and the complex rite of shuffling the dominoes begins.

There are thirty-two pieces in the game, comprising sixteen pairs of which some are identical and others slightly different from one another. First and foremost are the *Gee Joon*, the Supreme Creator pair which arise naked and alone within the primal void. The red and white dots painted so long ago onto the surface of the bone have faded to the point of near illegibility. We discern between them more by touch and essence than by sight. The game proceeds by intuition and sensation rather than by strategy. This is the method of those initiated into the mysteries of civil service.

After the *Gee Joon* come the stars, the earth, the first human couple, geese to eat and flowers to delight in, articles of clothing, benches on which to sit, even hatchets by which the geese may be slaughtered. Next come the children, and finally the military pairs, each member of each pair having a different number and arrangement of dots than does its twin. The entire collection represents the celestial court, a primal pattern which is reproduced at every level of creation. In our play, we court the ordinance of destiny, and thus we bring the fate of the Consulate into line with the dictates of the Embassy. We don't control our fate, we surrender it to something beyond us. The results of our operations cannot be known to us until they come to pass.

As the dominoes are shuffled, brick by ivory brick, I submit myself to the mantle of the presiding god. The swan descends upon me like a master who resides within a mansion in the heart of Heaven. She is sublime, yet aloof. She is subtle, even delicate, and yet She's as ruthless a strategist as any military general. She is above any consideration of mercy or compassion. Her attendant angels array themselves about me like a cabinet attending to their monarch. By the time the dominoes are shuffled, I am little more than a vessel for Her Holy Spirit. At length the hands are dealt and I make the first move.

The game stretches on into the late hours of the afternoon. An ecstasy of exhaustion overtakes us at length, a sensation with which I've become familiar over the preceding months. We're carried along a current insensible, borne upon a tide that has no origin. The waters satisfy our finer appetites just as they ravage the grosser of our senses. Again and again we plunge beneath the surface, losing ourselves in the vastness of an unintelligible depth, an ocean of communion in which all trace of the personal is lost. When we have finished, the bell is sounded once again. The results are meticulously recorded in the official logbook and the ritual furniture is put away. We avoid meeting one another's gaze. The state of intimacy brought about by our play is nearly overwhelming. So much as a moment's glance might pull us back into an embrace from which we would be powerless to extricate ourselves. It is only the rules and structures of the game, along with the didactic power of the indwelling god, that prevents us, during play, from overstepping our official bounds. Were it not for this, we might enter into a rapturous state of union which is strictly forbidden under international law. We are two and two we must remain, though we share a common essence.

In an hour's time, I'm walking through the front doors of the quaint little restaurant in which Edgar and I have agreed to meet. I'm late. Edgar has been kept waiting for quite some time. He sits at a table beneath the glow of a decorative lamp and moves the wooden pegs of a finely crafted game of *Solitaire* from hole to hole. His gaze rises to meet mine as I take the seat across from his. I'm exhausted. I must look a mess. It's clear, despite his utter lack of sensitivity, that he can sense the residue of my engagement with another man.

"The Consul must be pleased," he says, one finger resting upon a wooden peg while his chin rests on the other hand. "You work late hours for them at a moment's notice, and in return they pay you nothing."

"I'm an intern," I remind him. "That doesn't mean my work is unimportant."

"And what, precisely, does that work consist of?" he asks. "What oh-so-important service is it that you provide to them free of charge?"

"I'm paid in experience." We've been over this a thousand times before. "What I've learned at the Consulate will help me in the pursuit of my chosen vocation."

"What you've learned...?" The arrangement of pegs on the solitaire board, a really rather nice model, betrays Edgar's lack of strategy. He has no interest in the objective of the game. He simply wishes to exhaust every possibility of play as part of a prolonged study into the mathematical possibilities of the board.

"One of the drawbacks to pursuing a career in the civil service," I tell him, as if he doesn't know already, "is the discretion that must be maintained regarding the exact nature of my work. I would like nothing more than to speak openly about it, but I'm subject to certain restrictions."

We sit in silence for a full minute, a perfectly agonizing amount of time. He pretends to further study the board. The dark wooden pegs cast long shadows onto the surface of the soft maple. "You certainly burn through an excessive amount of gasoline," he says at last, his eyes still glued to the game. "One would think you simply drove in circles all day long."

"The commute is a little taxing," I concede. "I could take a bus, but public transport is woefully inadequate in the neighborhood in which I work."

A waiter comes to take our order. The better part of our meal is smothered in silence. He picks at his moules while I enjoy my lapin à la moutarde. "Perhaps I ought to contact Doctor Galloway," he mutters under his breath as he carefully rearranges the contents of his plate. I simply gaze at him impassively over the remains of my sumptuous feast. His remark doesn't even merit a response. Half a bottle of Beaujolais extinguishes the smoldering remains of his resentment. By the time we receive our dessert wines, he's back to his charming self again, regaling me with choice revelations turned up by his research. I'm inordinately grateful. After the day's exertion, I'm not sure how much of his derisive comments I can take without lashing into him.

Before we leave the restaurant, I'm made to understand that a surprise awaits me at home. I expect a new acquisition, a finely crafted game of rare distinction and antiquity. Imagine my delight upon crossing the threshold of the foyer to find a white cat, not much older than a kitten, stepping from the curved wooden backing of the davenport onto the lid which has been discreetly placed over the fish tank. The perfectly enchanting beast looks up as if to petition us to lift the cover that he might dip a paw into the water and retrieve a fish. I can't fail to notice that it bears a striking similarity to the cat that I saw outside of our hotel earlier in the week.

"Allow me to introduce you to the latest member of our household. Mrs. Chamberlain, meet Gershom Scholem."

"You *actually* named him Gershom Scholem?" I'm laughing now, incredulous and charmed all at once.

"Can you conceive of a better name for such a cunning animal?" He takes off his coat and hangs it in the foyer closet. "Anyway, they never come when you call for them, so we can name him anything we like. He climbed in through the window this morning while I was still immersed in study. He wears no collar and was as hungry as the devil (I gave him what remained of last night's swordfish), but he's awfully friendly and as clever as a Kabbalist. I think we ought to keep him."

I scoop him up into my arms and tickle his delicate paws with my fingers. There's no question that we'll keep him. I've already fallen for him.

In my dreams I wander through a busy port city bustling with administrative angels. Fiery ships filled with flaming missives arrive at the crowded harbor, setting fire to the docks and sending the city into a panic. Rolling clouds of smoke and soot besiege the sleeping masses, driving them from their homes into a countryside bathed in darkness. Tall white towers topple in the night, footbridges collapse in heaps of refuse, the walls of the houses of governance are shattered and their offices are destroyed. The venerable institutions are swiftly replaced with oracular machines built on ancient mines. As I return to wakefulness, the fleeting images cling to the surrounding darkness. They quickly fade as my eyes adjust to the dim light of the bedroom.

Again, my mouth is filled with the bitter taste of unidentifiable minerals, this time almost overwhelmingly so. In my mind's eye, I can see the ruins of the Library engulfed in flame. I haven't the slightest doubt that something has happened. I can no longer restrain myself. I must go to the Consulate and see what has transpired with my own eyes. I sit up in my bed to find Gersholm Scholem perched like a sultan on top of Edgar's sleeping body. The sleeper opens a single eye as I hastily pull on my clothes. "Go back to sleep, darling," I tell him. "I'll be back before you wake." He offers no reply. What could he possibly say to stop me?

I'm in my car before I've had the chance to fully awaken. I speed down the deserted, night-drenched streets, still enwrapped in the hazy fog of sleep. The stars hang overhead like vibrant chandeliers of ice, their bright bulbs bursting one by one as the flames overwhelm their containers. Streetlamps pass by overhead like drunken sailors on a desolate sea. My fingers stroke the gear shift as I leave the main road. My heart is racing, not with fear but with anticipation. I pass into a dark, tree-covered lane, accelerating around the winding curves with a minimum of caution. Images from my dream seep into the dark spaces beneath the boughs where the moonlight is swallowed up in shadow.

I arrive at the Consulate, parking my car on the side of the road at the approach to the tall gates. Having every expectation that they'll be locked, I prepare to scale the wall. As it happens, there's no need. The gate has been demolished. The wall has been blasted open in several places, as if by lightning. Chunks of misshapen masonry lie strewn about its base.

I step over twisted bars of tortured iron. The Consulate stands as secure as ever, majestic in its inviolability. The Library, on the other hand, is little more than a smoldering ruin. It looks as if it's been assaulted by a furious volcano. The roof, for the most part, is completely gone. One corner of the building has been smashed in. Large sections of the surrounding walls are missing. The indigo expanse of the sky can be seen through the many holes in the first floor ceiling. What remains of the attic lies naked and exposed to the impetuous glare of moonlight.

Of the two sphinxes that stand guard on either side of the stairs, one is simply gone, while the other has been smashed to bits. A single paw, the curve of the flank, and several fragments of a hind leg are all that is left of the once magnificent beast. The pedestal beneath it is still more or less in place, while the opposing pedestal has been overturned as if in a violent confrontation.

I approach the ravaged building with some measure of caution. I feel as if I have yet to emerge from the exacerbated landscape of my dream. It seems unlikely that I'm in any real danger. Whatever it was that launched the attack must be far from this place by now. A small white card lies in a pool of moonlight surrounded by debris on one of the stone steps. It's the card that I received from the official on my visit here while Edgar and I were still at the hotel. The image of the red-crowned crane stares up at me in perfect innocence, as if to ask of me what could possibly have happened in this place. I slip the card inside my purse, my burning curiosity growing with every passing second.

I am as awake now as I've ever been. Every nerve and muscle is poised for action. Forgetting for the moment any thought of my official duties, I ascend the steps and pass beneath the ruined arch that now comprises the Library entrance. The doors themselves are missing, as if they'd been ripped from their hinges and disposed of. I suppose they must be lying somewhere among the trees below.

I walk amidst the toppled shelves, cracked pedestals, and shattered glass. The smoldering remains of uncountable archives lie like fallen scribes about my feet. The relics of past ages, some several centuries old, are found scattered among the debris—warped and broken game boards, tarnished coins, and charred playing cards, among too many other things to mention. I recognize the remains of a particularly rare specimen from the Yuan dynasty. It had been on display behind two layers of glass in the lobby of the Consulate the first time that I'd set foot there. Now it lies in several pieces, barely recognizable.

While I cannot imagine who or what could have done this, I'm compelled to admit that the very thought of such power excites me. I have every reason to believe that the attack was at least condoned by the Ambassador, if not specifically carried out on his behalf. My thoughts turn to the card which now resides in my handbag, as well as to my illegal move on the *Xiangqi* board two days before. Am I somehow complicit in this incident? I feel as if I'm a pawn in a game that I can't possibly understand.

I make my way, with trepidation, to the upper floor of the ruined Library, ascending a staircase stained with soot from the first floor to the second. The attic is reached by the remains of a shorter, less ostentatious, stairway, previously concealed in the back of one of the archival vaults. The upper stairs have collapsed. I'm forced to pull myself up onto the unstable floor by one of the few remaining sturdy beams that protrude from behind the brick facade.

The wood beneath my feet is littered with half-burned pages and desecrated spines, all that's left of the extensive catalog of ancient rulebooks and the games that they described. Fragments of red and yellow reveal themselves in the moonlight beneath one of the mounds of charred paper. I bend down to investigate, plunging my hand into the refuse, staining my fingers with the leavings of our holy books. I pick up a game piece, an artifact that was spared from the attack. I quickly recognize it as one of my own, a piece that I'd stolen from Edgar's collection. It came from a reasonably well preserved *Chinesenspiel* set—the German 'game of the Chinese'. The game was made for children at a time when all of Europe was fascinated with the East, inspired by colorful tales of the Moghul empire and the wonders of their architects. The piece is large and cumbersome compared to the elegant designs of so many of my husband's games. The paint is flaking in several places, not because it's been damaged in the recent ordeal, but simply because it is very old. I hold it up to the moonlight, turning it over between my fingers as I examine its exquisite details.

It occurs to me that this particular piece owes its preservation to the fact that it doesn't belong here. I decide to use it as a talisman. It constitutes a link between the world in which my husband operates and the very different world of the Consulate. It follows that I should be able to make use of it to locate the threshold of yet a third world. I keep it firmly pressed against the palm of one hand as I make my way back down to the Library entrance.

One section of the wall that secures the grounds behind the Library has been reduced to a mound of crushed stone and debris. On the other side of the wall is a precipice, beyond which descends a long and sloping landscape almost entirely concealed in shadow. Hazy points of light can be seen in the distance beyond the incline. The expanse appears as if obscured by smoke. I'm only vaguely familiar with the area that I survey from my elevated position. I've passed through it once by railway, gazing out through the windows upon its narrow roads and endless fields. I don't imagine that it will be difficult for me to lose myself within its vastness.

With my leather clutch in one hand and the game piece in the other, I carefully proceed into the awaiting darkness. I'm immediately enveloped by the tall, somber trunks of innumerable trees drenched in shadow. Occasional shafts of moonlight penetrate the dense branches above, creating pools of iridescence which serve to nourish the finer of my senses. At times, when the foliage obscures the light completely, I'm forced to proceed by touch alone, passing from tree trunk to tree trunk with my hands outstretched before me. I continue in this manner for what must be hours. More than once, I nearly lose my balance and topple down the steep incline. I advance with no concern for my direction, having no fixed destination. I simply throw myself into whatever fate the Embassy has ordained for me.

Slowly, almost imperceptibly, the canopy of branches begins to thin as the sloping ground beneath my feet tapers to a more or less level expanse. My speed of travel increases. The trees that remain pass by like night watchmen, silently announcing the hours as the positions of their limbs betray their secret influences. Silver birches sway in the tepid night breeze, flexing their bedraggled fingers in impossible contortions. They seem to convey signals to the sycamores and field maples that pepper the increasingly spacious expanse. I let them gently guide my course as I penetrate ever further into their court. Their numbers diminish until the last pale trunk recedes into the distance, leaving me to advance in a climate of marvelous abandonment. The stretch of land before me is almost entirely obscured by shadows. Turning my gaze upward, I'm hardly surprised to find the constellation of Cygnus spread out across the sky. Everything below is drenched in rich, dark purple. I feel as though I've passed into a foreign country. The sensation of having crossed over a border is unmistakable, though I can't say precisely when it happened. My fingers stroke the game piece that still lies cupped within my palm. I occasionally turn it over between thumb and forefinger. It has an ethereal quality, as if it doesn't quite know what to make of itself. Its existence here is tenuous at best.

My progress toward the heart of this strange country is heralded by a flock of small, dark birds. I recognize the species as the Cape starling—native, if memory serves, to southern Africa. My training at the Consulate allows me to identify them with a reasonable degree of certainty. They swarm in from behind me with little warning, their disorienting symphony of mournful cries rising from the silence like a chorus of trumpets. Their bodies are bright azure, though their feathers incline in some places to indigo or even black. They swallow up the sky above me, occasionally revealing an opening through which can be seen a single star or a mutilated shaft of moonlight. As quickly as they'd arrived, they're gone again. They seem almost to disappear into a crack in the horizon.

Beneath the starling's fading cries can be heard the rumble of small explosions in the distance. The ground subtly trembles beneath me. The surrounding landscape is no longer empty. The rising flames of bonfires blaze on faraway hills as if to court a sky replete with shattered diamonds. I pass a row of broken down stone houses—hollow, desolate, and crumbling to dust. Beyond these empty habitations lie the ruins of what must at one time have been temples. Stark white altars stand upon the foundations. Some of them support brass bowls in which still smolder the remains of recent offerings.

Further still, a group of ravaged minarets rise from a labyrinth of ruined walls. I pass into their convolutions, stepping over low barriers of broken stone where passage is not otherwise possible. I set my game piece on a protruding ledge somewhere within the massive complex. Having crossed over into the place that I was seeking, it is no longer of use to me. The decaying walls resound with an exquisite sound of howling carried on the wind from the distant hills. These are doubtless the exalted cries of the missing sphinx that once guarded the Library, let loose without restraint upon an unfathomable environment in which its true nature is allowed to flourish and seethe.

The northern wall is largely intact, at least far more so than any other. I step out through a doorway and proceed to further wonders, quickly growing numb to the fascination they exert upon me. I've become indifferent to everything but the single object of my desire. The perfume of the Embassy enwraps my subtle senses. It kills my heart, smashes what's left of my sentiment, and continues to pull me ever further into its dark abyss. It saturates the ground beneath my feet. Even the air is heavy with its influence. I have no fear, no apprehension, nor any trace of trust or faith. What it is that I'm approaching is immune to worship or veneration, nor might it be supplicated or petitioned. The Embassy knows no morality—it's as ambiguous as it is opaque. I submit myself to whatever designs that its machinery may hold in store for me, not because I stand to gain from them, but simply because I am possessed of one inextinguishable ambition. The stone formations that pass by me, the howls and the distant thunder, the subtle wind that caresses my skin, even the incessant complaints of my aching limbs cease to register upon my senses. Neither my admiration for the Consul nor my love of my husband can retain their tenacity in the face of my pursuit. I divest myself of everything except the will to persevere.

I let the night devour me. I drown myself within its vastness. I'm propelled only by the incorrigible virtue that flames within my heart. The waters of obsession bear me up. I rise and surge upon the inflexible tide. It carries me forth and deposits me upon a shore at once unknowable and desolate. There they will find me, the Embassy's officials, washed up and broken on a foreign sand. From thence I will be carried inland, given shelter, a position inside the sanctuary. I will take my place as a frozen idol, distinguished, remote, and eternal, a single monument among a handful of others who have made it to the other side. After a lifetime of effort and careful positioning, I've made it at last to the immortal halls—the inviolable chambers of the Ambassador's dominion.

The Exalted and the Abased

Abasement

ONE blustery evening, a young man stood immobile for several agonizing minutes before a public house in Łódź. Its azure-painted entrance lay bathed in shadows in a shallow alcove beneath an overhanging bay window on Sierpnia Street. A single panel of frosted glass appeared in its upper face, its surface crossed by the whorls and arcs of an intricate wrought-iron grille. At the exact same time, a throng of workers were running amok in the Market Square in Kraków while National Socialists hatched insidious schemes beneath the lamps of a beer hall in Munich, yet the man, being entirely occupied with his own personal catastrophe, knew little of the shifting tides of influence and discontent that were sooner or later to erupt into another war.

The cause of the man's paralysis was his anticipation of a harrowing ordeal that awaited him in the apartment above. His increasing sensitivity to the penetrating cold eventually forced him into action. With a determined step forward, he pushed the door open with undue force, nearly colliding with a departing patron as he strode into the tiny vestibule. The two men begged each other's pardon and performed an awkward little dance until they'd managed to switch places, Florian stepping into the tavern's interior and his adversary into the larger embrace of the frigid November night.

A short trip beneath a row of chandeliers took him into the heart of the establishment. He chose a table near a corner that afforded him some privacy while allowing him to observe the surrounding décor. Candles of beeswax or, more likely, paraffin, cast pirouetting shadows from their niches in the walls. Their dim illumination vied with the radiance of the bulbs and their reflections on the mirrors that abounded in the place. An arch opened up in the wall behind the bar, just beyond which could be seen the lowermost steps of an ascending stairway. 'There,' thought Florian, 'if Tadeusz is to be believed, lies my passage to the house of the depraved.'

The lone attendant at work in the establishment made his way to Florian's table. He looked perfectly innocent in his professional attire. The copper buttons on his vest gleamed like enfeebled stars above his tarnished apron. His physical appetites were displayed in his demeanor like badges of honor. The satiation of desire was as natural to him as an act of prayer, the observance of which, so Florian assumed, he practiced with an assiduity that bordered on virtue.

"Would the gentleman like to order a drink?" he asked with an affected indifference.

"The gentleman, if he can so be called," answered Florian, "will not be drinking at all tonight. I've come seeking the more savory among the services of the house."

The bartender remained standing exactly where he was, the spectacles on his unshaven face reflecting the glare of the surrounding lights. Florian had desperately hoped that his cue would be picked up on. He would now have to explain, without all at knowing how, precisely what he'd come for. He thought the matter over for a moment, and, failing to come up with a suitable turn of phrase, decided on a more direct approach. "There is a woman," he said discreetly, "who I believe resides in the apartment directly above us, and whom I would very much like to meet."

"Am I to suppose that this woman has a name?" asked the impassive man.

"Her name is Kazimira, if I am not mistaken," said Florian, placing one uneasy hand over the other on the surface of the table.

"Very well," spake the bartender, as if Florian had ordered a glass of Krupnik. "I will put in a request with the lady in question and return to you with her reply."

Florian's heart sank a little as the attendant stepped away. He hadn't realized that there was any possibility that his inquiry might be refused. It occurred to him that the woman in question might have some method of observing him from her apartment, a hidden latch or spyhole in the floor that would allow her to determine his desirability as a client. A rush of self-consciousness surged through him as he attempted to shift to a more casual position. He wondered if he ought to have ordered a glass of something after all.

A photograph in a wooden frame on an adjacent wall caught his eye. He moved over on his bench a little in order to see it more clearly. A woman was shown seated on the edge of a divan covered by a length of silky fabric, its rolls and crevices revealing the contrasting shades of an intricate floral pattern. She was as naked as the limpid starlight save for a black and frilly shift which had been draped over one shoulder and across the landscape of her body. So furtive was her posture that she appeared about to slip away. Her eyes looked perfectly scandalous beneath the arch of her brow. Two white legs emerged from the lower fringes of her garment, her bare calves lying one atop the other like a pair of swans. A mirror in an ornate frame was raised in both hands before her, her face turned away from its surface as she looked to one side of the camera.

Florian was inexplicably struck with her denial of the mirror. He couldn't quite get it out of his mind that she had trapped her reflection inside of it. To turn her gaze to its reflective surface would be to place a key into a lock, bridging the divide between two worlds and freeing her imprisoned twin. He wished that he could shift the perspective of the image so as to allow him to view the glass. The implications behind its concealment were far more enticing than the woman's state of undress.

He turned his attention back toward the bar, half-expecting to find that the bartender, having neglected his request, had returned to his station to idle away the remainder of his shift. He was pleased to observe that the man was nowhere to be found. Moments later, he returned to the room from the descending stairway, emerging from the shadows of the arch with a sealed envelope in hand. This was deposited on Florian's table with a practiced flip of the wrist before the man departed without a word to tend to a row of empty glasses.

Florian turned the envelope over to find that it hadn't been sealed. He fished a stiff piece of paper from its interior, placing it face-up on the table before him. An illustration of the head and shoulders of a stern young woman greeted him, a single finger raised before her as if in admonition. Just below, in a flowery font, appeared the words: *For shame!* The rebuke stung his heart like the kiss of a whip, though he immediately felt foolish for allowing himself to be so affected. Turning the card over he found a message handwritten in scarlet ink: 'Do come pay me a visit. I'm in 207. Knock thrice and I will let you in.'

'Well, that was easy,' thought Florian. He read through the message a second time to ensure himself that he hadn't missed some subtle rebuff. He supposed there was nothing to do but proceed. Having no unfinished business to attend to in the lower section of the house, he rose from his seat without delay, sparing a final glance at the woman in the photograph before ascending to confront his debasement. He could feel her gaze boring into his back as he passed beneath the arch, her licentious demeanor setting fire to iniquities that lay dormant in his blood.

A brief ascent beneath a half-lit chandelier found him surprisingly composed. With each step, his trepidation diminished, as if his anxiety could not abide beneath the soft, golden glow that suffused the upper section of the stairs. Whatever trial lay before him took on all of the enticement of a rare and precious jewel. He wished to make of it an opiate, to drown himself within it, to let it poison his heart so that it might be resurrected in a fire for which he had no words.

He passed into a claustrophobic chamber that was scarcely larger than the vestibule downstairs. A single naked bulb set flame to the rough, brick walls, its effulgence resting like molten gold upon the dark, wooden panels of the two opposing doors. A brass plaque on the door to the left announced apartment 207. Florian executed a barely audible succession of raps upon the wooden surface.

Nearly half a minute passed in uncomfortable silence. It occurred to him that he still had time to make his escape into the night with his dignity intact. The flame of his cowardice was snuffed in its inception as the door swung open. He was greeted by a woman that must have been at least a decade older than was he. She stood with lips slightly parted, her shoulder pressed against the door frame, a cigarette held between two slender fingers. A crimson top clung tightly to her shoulders above a skirt of black lace that nearly reached her bare feet. She gazed at him for several seconds, her expression as unreadable as stone. "I suppose you'd better come in," she said at last. "You'll find it a little intimate inside, but it ought to be comfortable enough."

Florian dutifully followed her in and closed the door behind him. He was immediately confronted with a bewildering profusion of Chinese wood and decorative bottles. Innumerable shelves and cabinets concealed walls of understated saffron, their surfaces lined with glass containers filled with flower petals, bundled stalks, and desiccated roots and leaves. Thick books with weathered spines were stacked one atop another upon the crowded sill before the bay window. A pair of dark olive curtains concealed the view to the outside world. With a single gesture, Kazimira had Florian seated on a wooden bench beside the door, while she herself took up residence on an armchair of finely-carved mahogany. He carefully removed his overcoat and folded it in thirds, setting it down upon the floor beside him. He felt like an imposter in the intimate apartment.

"We might begin with a couple of preliminary questions," said the woman, her cigarette clasped between two fingers before the buttons on her blouse. "Do you understand the type of house you're in?"

From the moment he'd set foot in the apartment, Florian was afraid he'd made a dreadful mistake. The room's interior made him wonder if Tadeusz had misinformed him. While he would not do so intentionally, it was conceivable that his friend had misunderstood the nature of the establishment. Kazimira's question left him even more uneasy. If his answer was unsuitable, he might at once deliver her a dire insult and incriminate himself. He took a moment to consider his response, at length nudging the interaction forward as if he were making a move in a game of chess.

"I take it," he stated, somewhat more timidly than he'd intended, "that I'm not in an apothecary's studio."

The woman gave no indication as to whether his response was appropriate. She placed the cigarette between her lips, inhaled deeply, and blew out a torrent of harsh, white smoke, adding a hint of pungency to the mix of fragrances that suffused the apartment. "And are you familiar with the type of service that I provide?" she asked, her free hand cradled in the folds of her skirt.

"I have no reason to believe that I've been misinformed," he offered, uncertain how far this strategy would take him.

Her gaze betrayed a hint of suspicion, as if his answers had not been entirely sufficient. Of all of the possible outcomes, the one that terrified Florian the most was the one that seemed to be unfolding right before him. "I need you to tell me precisely why you've come," she said. "You must state it as plainly as you know how."

He tried to remember some of the phrases in the books that Tadeusz had shown him. The words conspired to trip him up, recombining in unacceptable formations that amounted to little more than nonsense. He knew it would be hopeless to try to frame his motivation in his own words. He lacked both the poetry and the self-assurance to give expression to his desire. At last, recalling a particular fragment that had struck him as especially poignant, he recited it as if by rote: "I wish to steal into the abbey in the heart of the night and crush the orchid at the foot of the altar."

Kazimira's demeanor considerably softened. "Good," she said. "That wasn't so difficult, now was it?" A rush of sweet relief flowed through Florian's every nerve. "Now," the woman continued, "try to put it in another way."

Just as his anxiety had begun to reassert itself, the words came to Florian's lips as if of their own accord. "I want to satiate my thirst with the milk of the abased and live to speak of it," he stated. As with the first, the phrase was vaguely remembered from the pages of a book. The words, when he'd first read them, had at once mystified him and aroused his curiosity.

"I would advise that you speak of it to no one," the woman returned. "Let your servitude proliferate in silence."

She rose, casually dropped the cigarette into a porcelain dish, and took herself to a curtain that concealed a section of the wall near the door. The heavy silk was pushed aside with a lazy sweep of the hand. A shallow niche resided in the space behind, its shelves containing a collection of implements that looked as if they belonged in a sacristy. A golden censer was retrieved from among a collection of chalices, cruets, and colored-glass lamps. This was transported to a work table beneath a crowded open cabinet. Kazimira turned her back to her guest as she continued her preparations, her fingers searching among several rows of labeled bottles above. Florian again had cause to wonder whether he'd come to the right place. He supposed it was best to simply play along. At worst he might embarrass himself, and anyway it wasn't as if he lacked the funds to pay for whatever services were rendered him. He watched in silence as the flower of a bright red poppy was taken from a metal bowl and placed onto a wooden tray next to the censer.

A match was struck, oils were poured, resins were collected and sparks flew from a disc of charcoal. For the most part, the movements of his hostess's hands were kept concealed by her body. His attention was distracted by a monochrome image that hung near the cabinet. Judging from the contrasts between light and shadow, it appeared to have been printed from a copper engraving. The artwork was framed in a square of stained wood. Its motifs were not unfamiliar to him. He'd seen something similar, if not exactly the same, within the pages of one of Tadeusz's books.

The image encompassed two interior spaces, the elements between them arranged with the economy of a Chinese puzzle box. The left-hand side featured an open archway, on the other side of which was found a woman dressed in an elaborate, flowing gown. She lay on her back upon a wide, stone bench, her expression betraying a calculating ill-will as if she were plotting her revenge against an unfaithful suitor. Through a window behind her, covered with an iron grill, could be seen a second woman in another chamber. The forefinger of one hand was raised to her lips while she passed a rolled-up slip of paper to an unseen recipient. The second woman was quite different from the first, appearing wholly devoid of subtlety or acumen, yet the furtive act in which she was engaged suggested otherwise.

The right half of the image showed a corridor that wrapped around from the space outside the arch. Here, a well-dressed gentleman sat cross-legged on the floor, his face turned toward a hardbound book that lay open on his lap. He was engrossed in the study of an illustrated cube that could just be made out on one of the pages. The man appeared fascinated by the simple geometric form. He displayed all of the single-mindedness of an idiot savant. As with the other two figures, his activity appeared to be purely symbolic, though the meaning of the symbols was anything but clear.

Florian recalled reading a detailed passage pertaining to this type of image. From what he remembered, it comprised a cabalistic device that had once been employed by lithographers and printmakers. The compositions were vaguely derived from variations of a single, little-known work—an eighteenth-century etching by a man named Basista, if memory served. Through the strategic placement of particular elements within a range of generic interiors the craftsman hoped to invoke the hidden laws of sympathy and correspondence. Thus did they intend to incite petty intrigues and misfortunes amongst their competitors and rivals.

His attention was torn away from the image as Kazimira turned around. Rising streams of sweet-smelling smoke emerged from a series of cross-shaped holes in the censer behind her. She'd unbuttoned her blouse and pulled back the fabric, exposing her naked breasts. She held the poppy flower with the fingers of both hands over her breastbone, the petals unfolding around the cluster of stamens as if to denote the central station of the sign of the cross.

Given the circumstances, it hardly seemed appropriate that Florian avert his gaze. He let himself observe his hostess as if she were a work of art. Her state of undress, though only partial, was like a statement of defiance. This was not the first time that he'd witnessed such things. He'd once attended a performance in Berlin that revealed far more than what was exposed to him now. This notwithstanding, there was something audacious about the unveiling of her flesh. Perhaps it was the intimacy of the little apartment, or the simple fact that the two of them were alone. In any case, he no longer doubted that he'd come to the right place.

After a moment of heedful contemplation on his part, Kazimira broke the silence. "Are you going to remain on your little bench all evening," she asked with disdain, "or are you going to get up and place your lips on the flower?"

Florian was naturally taken aback by the woman's effrontery. He hadn't the slightest idea what was expected of him. It was clear that she supposed him an experienced man. Though he knew it was ridiculous, the thought of revealing his innocence before her caused him an almost unbearable degree of anxiety. Intent on forging ahead on little more than pure bluff, he rose from his bench and took a cautious step forward. The admonition that followed nearly caused him to recoil.

"On your knees!" she insisted with a voice of vinegar and steel wool. She seemed genuinely displeased by his lack of protocol. "You must kiss it three times," she instructed, as if to a child. "No more and no less."

Florian did as he was told, lowering himself to the carpet with its swirling arabesques and inscrutable symmetries. The scarlet flower looked like a royal jewel against Kazimira's pale skin. He was dismayed, upon edging forward inch by inch, to find that the flower was too high for him to reach. "You may rise to a stoop," she informed him with a slightly less acerbic tongue. He felt it necessary to approach her with an exceeding degree of care. He had it in his mind that he was forbidden to touch her. To use his hands in any way, or to brush her flesh with either end of his mustache, would seem to constitute a violation of an inalterable rule.

Before he had a chance to bring his face to her breast, Kazimira began to softly intone a string of unintelligible syllables. Her vocalization was deliberately languid, her cadence so measured as to verge on monotonous. Her delivery, on the other hand, was so overwhelmingly sensuous that he was tempted to draw back from her. Her hymn, if it could be called as much, was anything but lacking in grace, yet for all of its refinement it concealed a core of corruption. A blossoming rose just past its prime was brought to mind, the tips of its petals slightly withered and discolored, the outermost among them falling prey to the early stages of decay. It occurred to Florian, to his slight distress, that this flower was his heart. It seemed explicitly opposed to the consecrated emblem that Kazimira pressed against her own.

As his lips approached the scarlet petals, Florian was given to a feeling of acute distress. It seemed to him as if the flower exposed something uncomfortably personal about the woman who bore it. It was suffused with the intimacy of a well-guarded secret, its carnality proclaimed by the dark eye at its center. The kiss itself, which was placed with the greatest care upon the central stigma, felt like nothing less than an obscenity. He was ashamed as he pulled his face away, the sweet scent of the flower having seeped into his palate. The feeling only escalated as he delivered another beneath the rising swell of his escort's voice. The second kiss felt even more explicit than the first, while the one to follow was accompanied by the ringing of a bell. Florian couldn't see how this was possible, as both of Kazimira's hands were fully occupied. Her intonation subsided in the wake of its reverberations.

"Now you must rise again," she said after a lengthy pause, the tone of her voice leaving no room for disobedience. Immediately as he did so, she stepped forward and embraced him, one hand placed in the small of his back while the other cradled his head with the poppy flower concealed in her palm. Florian's own hands extended to the impeccable territory of her waist. He drank of the intimacy between them as if it were a rare and precious wine. His previous hesitancy abruptly left him. More than a decade had passed since he'd been so close to a woman.

Kazimira's natural scent intoxicated him. So far as he could tell she wore no trace of perfume. She exuded a sense of self-possession that was pleasurably tinged with a hint of the erratic. He was shaken from the heat of her presence by the sensation of her breath upon his ear. "Exfoliate!" she whispered, before pulling her head back and gazing into his eyes. She moved as if to plant a kiss directly below his mustache, a gesture which he didn't hesitate to return. As their lips came into contact he felt a piercing shock of pain that caused his every muscle to grow rigid. His throat released a muffled shout like that of an animal in distress. She'd bitten down on his lower lip with such intensity that his vision had gone red.

"Good God, woman!" he exclaimed, when, after no more than a second, she released his skin from between her jaws. All at once, she withdrew her arms from behind him, giving him a gentle shove that sent him stumbling back onto the bench. He thrust both hands back to steady himself, awkwardly returning to a seated position. "You're like a pickpocket who thinks himself a jewel thief," she announced. "You ask for the night in all of its splendor, yet still you toy with the affections of the sun."

Having not a single clue what to make of her behavior, he simply gazed at his assailant with unconcealed resentment. He wasn't quite able to accept the turn that the evening had suddenly taken. He was bewildered and vaguely nauseous, his feelings thrown into disarray. "I'm bleeding now," he said indignantly, one hand raised to his injured lip. Had he his wits about him, he might have reflected that this sort of thing was not entirely removed from what he'd had in mind from the beginning.

"Good," rejoined Kazimira as she began to pull her blouse over her breasts. "The flow of blood is auspicious given the task that lies before you. I would suggest you staunch your wound this." One hand limply offered the poppy to Florian, who merely sat on his bench in contemptuous silence. The pain coursed through his jaw in shuddering waves. "I suppose you think I'm joking?" quipped the audacious woman, her hand waving the vibrant blossom in his direction. "There are particular operations in which the intermingling of fluids is an absolute necessity. This is one of them."

Florian reluctantly took the item offered him, keeping his gaze fixed on his hostess. Having nothing else to say to the woman, he lightly pressed one of the petals to his lip. Its contact, to his surprise, seemed considerably to numb the pain. The sense of prurience that was previously attached to it had entirely fallen away, leaving only its more exquisite qualities to mollify his discomfort. Now that he held it in his hand he was reluctant to relinquish it. Nevertheless, he handed it back beneath Kazimira's expectant gaze. The woman turned her back once more, the buttons on her blouse now securely fastened, and took the flower over to the work table. "The citadel of night awaits you," she assured him as her nimble hands set to work. "Whether you'll be granted entrance or turned away at the door remains to be seen."

Florian saw little point in offering a reply. His contact with the poppy had calmed his nerves in addition to quelling his pain. Thus far, the course of the evening's events had accomplished little more than to make him uncomfortable, yet he was compelled to admit that a door had been opened, a tiny germ of hope had been offered him. He wanted desperately to taste of waters that were not available to other men, to storm the chapel of forbidden experience and partake of unknown pleasures. What he truly desired, above all else, was to be relieved of the burden of being himself. Thus might he enter into an unfamiliar world that he was certain flourished right before his eyes, yet which had remained, for all of his thirty-seven years, entirely inaccessible to him.

After a couple of minutes, Kazimira turned to face him. A petite silver ball studded with evenly-spaced holes hung from a chain that dangled from her fingers. It was clear, from the scarlet fragments that could be seen through the apertures, that the poppy flower had been compressed and was concealed inside. "I will require of you but a single act of service," she said, as if with practiced casualness. "I need you to make a delivery to an associate of mine. Her name is Telesfora. I'll give you the address. There's a message for her here." She raised the sphere into the air before her. "The message is not intended for your eyes." Florian couldn't imagine how he might open the sphere even if he'd wanted to. No trace of a seam or latch could be seen from where he was sitting.

"You must make your delivery directly to my associate and no one else," Kazimira continued. "There are others in the house to which I'm sending you. They may very well attempt to deceive you. You must insist, and keep insisting, that the message be delivered in person. What she gives you in return will satisfy every measure of your desire."

"I understand," affirmed Florian, though in truth he didn't understand a single thing. He was dismayed at the prospect of seeking the services of yet another woman. At the very least, the development seemed inconvenient. What's more, he was a little afraid that their session was already drawing to a close. He'd been holding out the hope that what had happened so far was but a preliminary formality.

Kazimira had retrieved a card from one of the cabinet drawers. This, along with the metal sphere, was delivered to Florian's awaiting hands. An address was printed in unembellished black ink upon the surface of the card. His destination was not tremendously far. She appeared to be sending him to an affluent estate just off of Piotrkowska Street, little more than thirty minutes' walk from her apartment. He turned the paper over to inspect the reverse side only to find it blank.

Within the space of a minute, Kazimira was back on her bench enjoying another cigarette. She leaned her head back as she inhaled, sending the resulting jet of pale blue smoke into the air directly above her. "I believe our business here is finished," she said as she looked down to her client. "I don't have anything further to say to you."

Florian was thoroughly dismayed by her pronouncement. "Finished?" he uttered, somewhat exasperated. "But scarcely anything has passed between us!"

"Scarcely anything is needed," she rejoined, her heavy eyelids bathed in graceful pools of shadow. "You know precisely what the next step is. I trust I've made my instructions clear. I'll thank you now to vacate my apartment."

Florian began to wonder if he'd been taken in by an elaborate swindle before it occurred to him that the woman hadn't even mentioned the matter of payment. He supposed it was possible that the errand itself comprised Kazimira's fee. Still, the sting of disappointment felt like a laceration on his heart. He'd willingly put himself into an awkward situation and had received very little in return for his trouble. He rose and held the metal ball before him for a moment. His hostess smoked her cigarette and gazed toward the window. At last, conscious of the futility of trying to engage her further, he picked up his jacket, numbly put it on, slipped the item into one of the pockets, and headed out the door.

Exaltation

"You'll please excuse my intrusion. I have a parcel to deliver, it seems. For Telesfora. I'm afraid I've been instructed to deliver it directly to the lady in question."

"For Telesfora?" asked the woman, who was dressed in the uniform of a professional servant. Thick of frame and cloaked in dispassion, she occupied the narrow doorway like a church bell. "For Telesfora," he dutifully repeated, unable to regard the unpalatable maid as anything but an obstacle.

The woman simply stood in place, the lacework on her apron flipping to and fro beneath the caprices of the wind. "You'll have to wait a moment," she said at last, her expression never changing. "I suppose you ought to come into the foyer."

Florian was greatly relieved to be invited in. The weather was insufferable and the brisk walk had done little to warm his body. He followed the stolid woman inside, the metal ball with scarlet poppy tucked deep inside a hidden pocket. Though the entrance to the grand apartment was far from ostentatious, it was as pleasing to the soul as it was gracious to the eye. The maid continued through a wooden door flanked by panels of polished glass, brusquely closing it behind her as she disappeared into the inner reaches of the house.

Florian couldn't be bothered to seat himself on the chair in the corner. In any case, he wouldn't want his rain-soaked jacket to spoil the upholstery. A tasteful symphony of rich, red wood imparted an elegant allure to the little vestibule. The unintrusive glow of an overhead lamp bathed every surface of the space in amber flame. He allowed himself to peer through the glass panels set into the far door. Little could be seen in the space beyond save for a rising stairway.

It was a minor miracle that he was standing here at all. One thousand times, as he'd made his way to the apartment, had he nearly lost his nerve and simply took himself back home. He patted his left side with the palm of his hand to assure himself that the metal ball had not dropped out. Satisfied to find it still in its place, he cast an idle glance around the little room. A single item on a narrow table that stood against one wall caught his eye. Beneath a bulbous wineglass half-filled with water lay a square of thick, white paper. Though the central section was obscured, Florian immediately recognized the stylistic motifs that he'd seen framed on Kazimira's wall. Unable to resist his curiosity, and hoping to God that he wouldn't be caught, he slipped his fingers beneath the bowl of the glass and lifted it just enough to examine the design below. What he found was exactly as expected—the layout of the piece was notably different from the one he'd examined earlier.

Though the setting had been changed, the aesthetic was the same. A single room was shown from an angle, while two broad doorways set into either wall afforded views into what appeared to be completely different areas. The well-dressed man, in the center of the image, was seated at a work desk before an ornate candlestick. He'd wrapped one hand around the rising taper while his gaze remained fixed on the flame. On one side of the candle sat a draughtsman's compass and on the other a leather glove.

The other two figures could be seen through the doorways. The woman in the flowing gown was shown gazing into a mirror on the right-hand side. It was impossible to tell from the angle of the glass, but there appeared to be no reflection. The second, more plain-ly-dressed woman, on the opposing side of the image, was shown placing a key into a heavy wooden door. In the upper section of the door was found a small, barred window. She peered through the opening at what was presumably a fourth figure, though the latter was ob-scured by the perspective of the image.

The composition must have been one of dozens based on Basista's original, each one featuring its own subtle differences and endowed with unique signifi-cance. The way in which it had been left in the foyer brought to mind the protective amulets one sometimes found attached to doors throughout the city. He suspected it had been placed there to protect against thieves or to ward off the ill-will of quarrelsome neigh-bors. The maid seemed like the most likely culprit. She struck him as the superstitious type. He could imagine her choosing from a catalog of charms based on the phases of the moon or the positions of the stars. What purpose the device might have served on Kazimira's wall was another question entirely.

At the sound of approaching footsteps, Florian swiftly placed the glass back down and slipped his hands into the pockets of his overcoat. The inner door swung open to reveal nothing more than the maid, her hair tied back in a tidy little bun above her slightly boorish brow. "Mirosław will see you now," she duly informed him. "He awaits you upstairs." Her overbearing presence was as delicate as a canon.

"I'm afraid I've been specifically directed to deliver my message by hand," he returned, feeling a little like a secret agent exchanging a coded pass-phrase.

"That isn't any of my business," she said. "I'm merely following orders." Florian could see that he may as well attempt to reason with the wallpaper.

With a dutiful step, she turned around and passed back through the door. He followed after her into a well-designed main hall beneath the melancholy auspices of several hanging lamps. Polished wooden panels housed lighted displays featuring paintings of men in impeccable uniforms. They sat atop horses with their troops arrayed about them and their blades raised high above their heads. The whole gave the impression of a bastion of peace amidst an endless parade of military showmanship. Florian had seen the aesthetic before. It conveyed all of the warmth of a petrified flame. The two of them ascended to an upper landing before a doorway flanked by two wall-mounted bulbs. From there, they passed into a dignified suite that seemed to reside at the apartment's heart.

A man, presumably Mirosław, awaited them beneath a soft cascade of lights. He sat in one of two matching armchairs at the far end of the room. A carpet before them overflowed with a symmetrical design of black and crimson, its pale fringes gleaming against the dark wooden floor. Behind him stood a console table beneath a colossal, gold-framed mirror. The head of the stairs could just be seen in the reflection, giving the uncanny appearance of a second stairway that led down into a secret region in the back of the house.

"Do please sit down," said Mirosław, who seemed conspicuously overdressed for such an unexpected call. Florian wondered if perhaps he'd been awaiting more illustrious company. It was assumed, both by his manner and the style of his house, that he worked as a public official. He had about him the familiar reserve of those that had served beneath a succession of administrations. Florian indulged the man's request, not troubling himself to remove his overcoat. He felt tremendously ungracious as he did so, yet he was determined to avoid relinquishing his hold on the item he was sent to deliver.

"Shall I have Jadwiga fetch something for you?" asked the decorous man. "We keep a well-stocked cabinet, though we rarely indulge."

Florian thirsted for a dry Muscat, but, thinking it best to keep focused on his task, politely refused. Mirosław introduced himself as such after dismissing the maid. Florian did the same in return as she made her exit.

131

"If I'm to understand, you have a message for our Telesfora?" offered Mirosław, the fingers of one hand toying with the inseam of his silken vest.

Florian merely nodded his ascent, vaguely self-conscious that the blemish on his lip would make him appear a ruffian.

"I'm afraid the good woman is indisposed at the moment," said Mirosław in a voice tinged with regret. "I'll be happy, however, to see to it that your message is received without undue delay."

"Therein lies the difficulty, I'm afraid," said Florian. "I was specifically instructed to deliver my message by hand. In person. You'll understand my dilemma."

Mirosław slipped two fingers between a pair of buttons at his breast, giving no sign of acknowledgement as to the requirement of his host. "And whom might I presume the message is from?" he asked.

"From Kazimira," uttered Florian, as if the woman's given name was a household word.

"I see," said Mirosław, his eyes shifting briefly downward toward his lap. Florian did his best to keep his gaze from wandering. He yearned to steal a glance into the corridors and chambers that were partially revealed through the open doorways to either side. The sparsity of furniture gave him little else with which to distract his attention. The lack of any view to the outside world made him feel distinctly isolated as he tried to find a comfortable position in his armchair.

Mirosław resumed the conversation, if on a slightly unexpected tack. "I take it you're aware," he said, "that common men and women are now rioting in the streets of Kraków?"

Florian didn't know quite what to say. He rarely kept abreast of current events. For the first time since he'd entered the apartment, he felt at somewhat of a loss for a response. He raised his fingers to his lower lip, lightly brushing his minor wound as if it were somehow responsible for the disturbance his host was referring to. "I don't know anything about it," he returned at length, placing his hand back in his lap. "I'm sure it isn't any of my business."

Mirosław rested both of his hands palms-down upon the arms of his chair, the pale fire of the lamplight tracing serpentine paths along the traceries on his vest. "The Market Square is being overtaken with seditious workers as we speak," he reported. "They've sent in soldiers on horseback, but their hooves are next to useless on the rain-soaked tiles. The rabble is attacking them without pity or remorse—seizing the policemen's rifles, shouting out the lyrics to *The Internationale*, occasionally fleeing into nearby houses only to open fire on the presiding officials from the upper-story windows. In a recent development, they've managed to take control of an armored vehicle. The driver was killed and his body thrown down before the eyes of an astonished crowd. It's a terrible business, an unmitigated catastrophe—a blossoming of the unspeakable in the midst of a well-ordered city."

Florian had only been dimly aware of the tensions developing among the lower classes. The railroads, he knew, had recently been militarized in response to a rising tide of worker provocations. Minor incidents were reported on a nearly constant basis. Just the day before, according to the newspapers, the Socialist Party had proclaimed a general strike. He hadn't paid the troubles even the slightest bit of mind. He was comfortable enough in his middle-class existence, maintaining a reasonable living as a general manager in a translation office. He wondered how this man Mirosław could possibly know so much about events that were unfolding as they spoke. He must have contacts that kept him well informed and up-to-date. The greater question was what any of this had to do with the purpose of his call. He couldn't help but feel that he was being manipulated in some way.

"I must admit to a total ignorance of the affair," he conceded after a moment of silence, unable to produce a more relevant comment. "It is troubling, to be sure."

"Are you certain I can't offer you a drink?" asked Mirosław a second time.

"I think it would be best if I refused," returned Florian, feeling it wise to cling to prudence as if it were a life-raft.

"An understandable choice," said Mirosław. "The office of messenger is not to be taken lightly, after all."

Florian felt as if he were taking part in a carefully plotted game. The exchange thus far had something of the flavor of a perfunctory charade. Every word, every gesture, every facial tic and innuendo seemed to him suffused with hidden significance. He felt a trace of dismay at the passivity of his role. He suspected that he'd already failed in the task that he'd been charged with. If he could only distract his host's attention, so he fancied, he might slip into the mirror and abscond down the stairway that he'd spotted in the reflection. His reverie was broken by the unsettled monotony of Mirosław's voice.

"I'm not entirely certain that I made myself clear when I said that Telesfora was not available," he said. "I'll do my best to explain the situation in more succinct terms."

The man took a moment to compose his thoughts, momentarily running two fingers down one side of his clean-shaven face. With little pause, he turned again to address his guest.

"The principal function of the night is to conceal, is it not?" he offered, as if his assertion was self-evident. "It draws a veil of obscurity over our most venerable institutions—it even, for the most part, keeps us hidden from ourselves."

A tiny wave of sadness rushed through Florian's heart like a tenuous and unruly flame.

"There are houses of influence that can only abide in utter darkness," the man continued. "They play a decisive hand in current affairs, though they rarely act in unison. Their officials and administrators are notoriously difficult to reach, requiring long-outmoded channels and undocumented protocols. On occasion, one of them is forced to take measures that have dire repercussions—the unfortunate business in Kraków is one of countless such instances. While the authority exerted from behind their closed doors is nearly incomprehensible, it's known to have its limits. The methods employed are as fallible as any other."

Mirosław paused for a moment, his eyes glancing down at the surface of the carpet as if the weight and direction of his monolog might be derived from its elaborate symmetries.

"What can we possibly know of the shifting tides of fate on which all of Europe is tossed hither and thither?" he pondered. "The decisions made under the cover of the night are the result of incalculable factors. It's best not to speak of such things. I wouldn't mention them at all but for the sake of justifying Telesfora's unavailability."

"I'm not entirely certain I follow," said Florian, having almost forgotten his reason for coming.

Mirosław leaned forward, enunciating softly and with care as if conveying a matter of tragic importance to a child. "Telesfora is with the Minister of the House of Abnegation," he said. Again he paused, considering his words. "In spirit, I mean."

Florian wondered if Mirosław was trying to convey to him that the woman was deceased.

"The means are available to me of seeing to it that she receives whatever messages are intended for her," the man continued. "I have in my possession a document of passage signed by all the necessary hands. The process is not entirely without its dangers, yet I find I must make use of it from time to time. It is expedient, if nothing else."

A burst of sudden inspiration arose in Florian's breast. It almost felt as if it had its origin in the metal ball concealed in his inner pocket. "May I see it?" he asked, leaning forward in his armchair for the first time since he'd seated himself.

A look of perplexity crossed over Mirosław's face. He seemed genuinely unsure what to say in response. "I beg your pardon?" was all he could come out with, as if his guest had spoken out of turn.

"The document you spoke of," asserted Florian. "If it isn't too much trouble, I'd be interested in looking it over. I feel it's my responsibility as official messenger. One must assure oneself that all is in proper order, after all."

Mirosław could see that he was clearly at a loss. The thread of conversation had been irreversibly severed. His dismay bespoke the gravity of the situation—it was as if a crucial misstep had thrown his would-be waltz into a fumbling lurch from which he couldn't quite recover. His expression betrayed an attempt to strategize his way back into the upper hand. After a brief delay, his features again softened. It was clear that he'd resigned himself to conceding his advantage.

"Of course," he said, one hand raised slightly before him. "It's not the least bit of trouble. You'll have to wait while I retrieve it, but I won't be long."

Florian merely bowed his head, partly in condolence, as Mirosław rose and clasped his fingers upon a button on his vest. For a fraction of a second, he looked entirely lost. He smoothed the surface of his silken tie, turned himself around, and headed out the open doorway nearest to his chair. Upon hearing his opponent's footsteps receding in the distance, Florian swiftly rose to his feet and darted off in the other direction.

The doorway that he'd chosen looked more or less the same as any other. In any case, he hardly had the luxury of discriminating. His sole aim was to locate Telesfora as quickly as possible. Once the item had been delivered, it hardly mattered what became of him. In any case, he felt reasonably assured that she'd protect him from the repercussions of his rashness. He only hoped that she was indeed to be found somewhere inside the house, and further, that she was in an appropriate state to receive Kazimira's message.

His progress down the adjoining corridor was cut short by the soft thud of approaching footsteps. From the sound of it, they were still a reasonable distance away. Jadwiga, for it was doubtless she, must have been coming from somewhere around the bend. Her plodding step was unmistakable. His first thought was to dash back down the stairs and flee into the shelter of the cold, November night. Instead, he stepped into a doorway to one side with as little noise as he could manage.

The chamber he'd stepped into was abundantly lit. It looked just like an accountant's office with its compact work desk and overstuffed bureau. He pressed his back against the inner wall, satisfied that no trace of his shadow was cast across the doorway. The approach of the maid felt like a swiftly advancing tide as she rounded the hallway corner. Florian was certain that her presence would engulf him, that he would be drowned beneath the magnitude of her all-encompassing physicality. He didn't dare to look behind him as she passed by the open door. When at last she turned and began again to head away from him, he nearly collapsed onto the floor in relief.

He kept perfectly still for several minutes after the sound of her footsteps had diminished, unable to escape the unnerving feeling that she was somehow still lingering on the far side of the door. The trappings of the office were sufficient to distract him, at once calming his nerves and inciting his curiosity. The desk was covered with thick squares of paper of the same size as the one in the foyer. Each was fronted with an illustration in the style of Basista. Drawing rooms, cellars, corridors, and winding stairs were peopled by all of the familiar characters, each of them enacting a multiplicity of rites with the aid of perfume bottles, handheld fans, daggers, playing cards, spectacles, dice, and coiled leather whips. Though they rarely interacted with one another directly, they seemed tenuously connected by countless narrative threads. The significance of their activities remained always just short of cohesion, as if each of the scenes comprised half of a parable while the other half remained in the dark.

The bureau that stood against the far wall was open just a crack, unable to close for the excess of items stuffed inside. From what he could see, these, too, were comprised of variations of the talismanic print. A moment's observation revealed that the same was true for at least one of the desk drawers as well. Assuming each one was unique, there must have been thousands of them. Florian assumed that each of them was intended to address a particular desire, whether for protection, revenge, persuasion, or affluence.

It occurred to him that if only he knew how he might make use of the images himself. If properly applied, they might help him track down Telesfora while avoiding an encounter with either Mirosław or the maid. His lack of acumen with operations of this type left him feeling like a child. He was far too inhibited to make a study of the kinds of books that Tadeusz was conversant with. While he was fascinated with the arcane, the cabbalistic, the irrational, there was something about their elusive mystique that left him feeling hopelessly inadequate. This was indeed one of the reasons that he'd initially sought out Kazimira's services.

Just to one side of the bureau, opposite the corridor, was found a pair of doors so unremarkable that his eye had previously passed right over them. While he was satisfied that Jadwiga was nowhere near the office, he was wary of returning to the corridor. Hardly expecting to find them unlocked, he stepped over to the doors and cautiously tried one of the white-painted handles. He was delighted when the door swung open without the slightest trace of resistance.

The space beyond revealed a modest, yet well-decorated chamber. A quick sweep of the eyes from one end to the other assured him of his solitude. His new environment was far more enticing than the one in which he'd met with Mirosław. He would appear to have found his way into an intimate assembly room beneath the auspices of a single chandelier. Ornate cabinets of imported wood looked down onto a collection of Moroccan armchairs, their upholstery aflame with serpentine lattices that shimmered and pulsed beneath the glow of the light. They were arranged as if for an audience of no more than six or seven, their backs turned to an alcove on the far end of the room. A little door of black lacquer was set into the recess, its upper panel inset with a carved wooden screen of the type that one might find in a confessional booth. On the opposing wall, behind a podium of dark-stained chestnut, hung a banner of finely-woven silk.

Ever-conscious of the need to keep moving, yet in no hurry to retrace his steps, Florian closed the door behind him with a remarkable lightness of touch. He was curious to examine the image displayed on the upper half of the banner, the outlines of which were traced in vibrant orange on a background of deep sapphire. The reflection of the lights on the shimmering fabric brought out the contrast between the two colors, causing the delicate line work to pulse and scintillate as if with an electrical charge. As he let his gaze go slightly out of focus, the composition emerged into full visibility.

Perched upon a rising slope, amidst a devastating gale, was shown a gargantuan monstrosity of brick and stone in the rough form of a cube. Vibrant bursts of golden light emerged from the windows in its upper stories, surrounding the edifice in a resplendent glow that seemed to emanate from its concealed heart. Countless items had been picked up by the winds and whirled aloft around the outer terraces and pilasters. Whole trees had been ripped clean from the earth, their trunks inverted or snapped into pieces while their flailing limbs were put to the mercy of the caprices of the storm. Other items had been sucked up into the dizzying spiral as well—a church steeple, a chariot wheel, a door torn from its hinges, a terrified man wrapped up in an overcoat, and a pair of oxen with their hooves raised in the air. The building itself remained fixed to the ground amidst the tumult of the elements, the malicious blows of the howling winds assaulting it in vain.

The colors on the banner were so vivacious that they overwhelmed the surrounding décor. They flashed with an intensity that made the winds appear as if they were truly in motion. The illusion was heightened by the play of the lamp on the surface of the silk. There was no question that it was intended to dazzle whoever might reside on the chairs below. Florian wondered if the building was intended to depict one of the "houses of influence" that Mirosław had spoken of. At the time, he'd assumed that his host had been making fun of him.

As he continued to study the finer details of the image, he noticed a curious inconsistency in the walls of the edifice. The uneven lines in which the stones were depicted made them appear as if they were transparent. It was almost as if he could see right into the interior of the house. A closer look revealed a perplexing labyrinth of corridors, chambers, and winding stairs, all peopled with phantasmal figures engaged in a variety of pursuits. He was able to make out repeated depictions of Mirosław and the maid, each of them occupied in rites and machinations involving household objects and commonplace implements. Telesfora, if that was who the other woman was, was found only once, though she appeared to move from place to place. The paths of the inhabitants never seemed to converge, though their activities intersected with the consistency of clockwork. Florian caught glimpses of himself as well, forever seeking to escape his pursuers as he attempted to deliver his message. One by one, he evaded their schemes, yet Telesfora remained unreachable, seeming ever to abscond to a region of the house roughly opposite his own position.

He was brought out of his minor trance by the sound of footsteps in the corridor outside. So acute was his return to his physical environment that he could feel the blood coursing through his veins. The fluids in his body seemed to pulse in sympathy with the object given him by Kazimira, its subtle intoxicants dispersing through his system like the slow unwinding of ink in water. His pursuers would seem to be swiftly approaching. This time the heavy, inelegant gait of the maid was accompanied by the efficient step of Mirosław himself. In a panic, he dashed around the chairs toward the alcove at the back of the room. The black-painted door, to his great relief, swung open without the slightest resistance. His fingers fumbled for a lock of some type as he concealed himself in the darkness beyond. The official and his servant made their entrance within seconds of the latch sliding quietly shut.

Florian's view through the wooden screen was frustratingly limited. He stood as rigid as a streetlamp, remaining just far back enough to avoid detection, yet close enough to see into the other room. Both the podium and banner were within his line of sight, though neither Mirosław nor the maid could be seen. He felt certain that one of them would think to check behind the door. His heart was beating so erratically that he feared its pounding alone would give him away. He considered the possibility of bursting out on them in order to take them by surprise. How far, he wondered, might he retreat into the house before they came to their senses and started after him?

"Here we are then," said Mirosław, the timbre of his voice accentuated by the acoustics of the tiny chamber. "It appears as if our little bird has flown back into the night."

"I suppose so," answered Jadwiga. "It seems unlikely that he could have made it to the upper story of the house without crossing at least one of our paths." It sounded like she was standing within arm's reach of the alcove. Her employer, for his part, would seem to be stationed near the double door.

Florian couldn't help but notice, for the second time now, that Jadwiga had far stronger of a presence than did Mirosław. While the latter came off as a crafty man who was able to change his allegiance as needed, his servant was possessed of a substantial inner fire that was as constant as the sun. He could feel the weight of her cumbersome vitality from his place in the closet. It seemed to seep into his body and intoxicate his blood.

"Nevertheless, there's a chance he's still in the house," said Mirosław after a moment of silence. "We'd best take due precautions and have him driven out."

"I'll have it taken care of straight away," replied Jadwiga in a voice as stoic as a marble slab, the ties at the rear of her apron dangling just within view.

Florian couldn't begin to imagine what manner of ruse they were playing, though he suspected they knew perfectly well where he was. Something about their brief exchange had struck him as artificial. He couldn't quite believe that they'd neglect to check behind the door. He was fully prepared to barricade himself within the darkened space if need be. It wasn't as if he'd had time to come up with a more reasonable plan.

Jadwiga remained as if rooted in place as Mirosław made his exit, her natural torpor suffusing the chamber like an unsavory perfume. Florian dared to take a half-step forward, though this did nothing to improve his view. He briefly wondered if there were other servants that worked in the house as well, though his intuition told him that she worked alone. He imagined her proceeding from one room to another, lighting candles atop squares of paper and muttering formulae beneath her breath. The use of such an arcane device must have provided some relief from the tedium of her job.

He relaxed a little, despite himself, as her apron strings passed out of sight. She appeared to be headed back toward the double door. He didn't want to get his hopes up. It was clear that he was trapped. Again, he felt the sting of failure piercing his heart like a thorn. If only he could manage to get out of the apartment, he might still find a way to complete his task. He could always track down Telesfora sometime later on the streets of Łódź. Kazimira had said nothing about delivering the message in a timely manner. His thoughts on the matter were abruptly cut short as he was plunged without warning into total blackness.

The loss of his sight put him entirely at Jadwiga's mercy. Though it was clearly she that had switched off the light, she seemed in no hurry to leave the assembly room. He could hear her rummaging about in one of the cabinets affixed to the near wall. The intimacy that arose from her proximity, along with the fact that he was hidden in the dark, made him feel like a schoolboy that was spying on a superior from a place he was forbidden to set foot.

The sudden darkness was followed by an unexpected flare of light. A flaming taper in a copper candlestick was set down on one side of the podium. It was joined by another a moment later, the twin lights tracing shimmering arcs across the surface of the silken banner. The image printed on the fabric appeared to pulse and waver through the apertures in the wooden screen. Florian was afforded only a moment's view before the heavyset woman positioned herself directly between the flames.

A knock upon the podium was followed by several seconds of silence. It was difficult to tell with his limited view, but it appeared as if Jadwiga was tracing figures in the air before her with the fingers of one hand. A hushed rustle of whispered syllables softly wafted through the chamber. A wave of unease washed through Florian's conscience, as if he were witnessing a pornographic act. With an unexpected grace, Jadwiga leaned back her head and raised her arms to either side. As quickly as they'd started, her whispered incantations ceased. In their wake arose a melodious chant that bore a striking resemblance to the one he'd been subjected to earlier.

If the hymn delivered by Kazimira could be likened to a vintage of debauch, this woman's was like a vast, insipid ocean. Nothing explicit in her voice suggested the slightest trace of vehemence, yet the syllables rolled forth with a relentlessness that wounded him. Jadwiga wielded her reverence with the precision of a battering ram. Florian was filled with an irrational fear that somebody outside would hear her. The intonation continued to rush through him like a mortifying tide. Closing his eyes only intensified his shame. By fixing his gaze on the candle flames, he was at least able to keep his bearings. He pressed himself up against the back of the door, his fingertips seeking the sensation of the wooden screen. There was little he could do but passively await the end of the ordeal.

He was finally given some respite as the litany dwindled to a halt. Jadwiga hastily stepped away from the podium, affording her prisoner a full view of the banner in the flickering light of the candles. Florian wasn't sure whether she'd remained in the assembly room or had made her exit through the adjoining office. His attention was entirely enwrapped in the image of the wind-encircled house. The unsteady lines that comprised the artwork were given further animation by the dance of the flame. The building's interior shone through the walls like a film projected onto stone. Again, he witnessed multiple instances of Mirosław and the maid. They passed from one place to another like a cadre of spies, their allegorical narratives unfolding in accordance with a mesmerizing symmetry. As he became increasingly drawn in by their intricate formations, his surroundings fell away from him like the petals of an orchid. He took his place within the labyrinth as if immersed in a waking dream.

He passed through corridors and antechambers, crept down long and winding stairs, and traversed a series of meandering crawl spaces in a continual effort to evade his pursuers. Every conceivable stratagem was employed to deceive him, seduce him, or otherwise lead him into Mirosław's hands. With a finesse presumably bestowed on him by the talismanic flower, he managed to outmaneuver every one of them. At length, after an interminable pursuit, he emerged into an upper chamber. What he witnessed in the magnificent space comprised the jeweled heart of the entire institution.

Elaborate panels of polished brass described a circle around the room. Torches had been raised around the perimeter, their flames tracing intricate forms along the curved, metallic surfaces. Limpid starlight filtered in through an elaborate dome of transparent glass. In the center of the chamber stood a mechanical contrivance of considerable size. It was conical in shape, its wide, circular base growing narrower as it ascended to a point. Its ivory surface was encircled by a series of spiraling grooves that wound their way toward the peak. The narrow canals emitted pulsating light in a variety of colors. From its heart emerged an electrical hum that seemed to infiltrate the corridors and chambers below. There was something almost magisterial about the inscrutable device. It was clear that it maintained the inner workings of the house with a meticulous degree of precision.

By the logic that predominates in dreams and visions, Florian knew precisely what the apparatus was. He was standing in the presence of nothing less than the Minister of the House of Abnegation. The resonant drone that emerged from its interior began to rise in pitch. It seemed to surge up through the grooves that wound their way around its surface, steadily ascending in fluctuating waves. Though the Minister was purely mineral in substance, its indwelling presence set the atmosphere aflame. Within seconds, its wail had risen so high that it could no longer be contained.

With a tumultuous crash, the panels in the dome above shattered all at once, showering both the Minister and the floor with flying shards of glass. A violent gust from outside of the house swept into the chamber's interior, swiftly extinguishing the surrounding torches and throwing the furniture into disarray. Projectiles of glass passed through Florian's body as if he were a ghost. He crouched low to the floor before the ivory pyramid as its incessant whine continued to escalate. The flashing lights still swarmed along its surface like a revolving horde of Seraphim. A selection of brass panels were ripped loose from their foundations by a blinding crack of lightning, its brilliance revealing a dizzying view of the horizon outside the house. For a single moment, as pale fire filled the sky, the darkened landscape was illuminated in full.

Two colossal figures could be seen in the distance before a dark blue mountain range, their bodies leaving an imprint on the background of Florian's field of vision. The first, a woman of undeniable authority, was clad in a flowing scarlet gown. She raised a scourge above her head in one hand while the other grasped the lightning like an ancient Greek goddess. She gazed in unconcealed contempt upon a pitiable man that cowered on the ground before her. The latter, who wore little more than a loincloth, had his brow pressed down to the cold, dark earth. He'd been thoroughly humiliated and debased. His back looked like an open field after the Battle of the Somme. Long, dark rifts lay arrayed like trenches across the landscape of his flesh. Florian immediately understood that the man was an aspect of the Minister. While the inscrutable machine asserted its prestige from the peak of its house of governance, its dark twin ran feral in the wilderness outside. The woman, there could be no doubt, was Telesfora herself, her body caressed by the scintillating radiance of heaven's fleeting fire.

Florian remained huddled in the darkness after the lightning flash had passed, the trenchant hum of the presiding machine slicing through him like a razor. He felt as if he'd at last found his way before the altar in the sleeping abbey, yet the flower that was crushed at its foot was not his own. The milk of abasement and the splendor of the night remained perfectly indifferent to his meaningless quandaries. He couldn't begin to comprehend the impossible forces commanded by the woman with the scourge. The sight of her exquisite cruelty had filled the basin of his senses to the point of overflowing. The pyramid, the blasted dome, and the house that extended below him were washed away in an unstoppable deluge of confusion and desire.

He couldn't say for how long he remained in his insensible state. By the time the waves rolled back and he'd returned to himself, the candles on the podium were nearly halfway burned down. His brow was pressed uncomfortably against the apertures in the wooden screen. He must have been entranced for hours. Hardly inclined to shift his position, he simply stood in place and listened to the soft rasp of his breathing in the dark. He felt like a boy who'd wandered into a brothel and encountered something unspeakable. What he'd witnessed had marked him like the lash of a whip.

Snippets of his meeting with the Minister continued to revolve in his imagination, the sights alighting on his inner vision like the play of light on water. His internal landscape was still aflame with the effulgence of the lightning. Additional areas outside the house emerged from the depths of his memory, features that had escaped him while his attention was fixed on Telesfora. The mountains had been rife with temples devastated by the wind. Half-collapsed towers and smoldering basilicas had peppered the uneven plain. He vaguely remembered catching sight of the oxen that had been lifted off the ground by the gale. The entire region had been reduced to a storm-ravaged wasteland.

Several uneventful minutes passed as he gradually came back to his bearings. At length, he found the strength to move again, stepping back from the door and straightening his spine. It was impossible to tell by peering through the wooden screen whether Jadwiga was still in the room outside. The prospect seemed unlikely. The space was suffused in the hush of solitude. Given the lateness of the hour, it seemed reasonable to assume that the denizens of the house had gone to bed. He stood in place throughout the course of sev-

151

eral shallow breaths before he dared to slip the latch and open the door. Upon stepping out, he was greatly relieved to find himself alone in the flickering light of the candle flames.

He cast a sheepish glance up at the banner behind the podium. The house, the storm, and the flying detritus appeared as flat and unremarkable as a newspaper sketch. The whirling bodies flailed wistfully about like figures in a comic strip. No trace of the interior of the edifice could be seen. He was given to the notion that, having so recently passed into the inner reaches of the house, he was immune for the time being from doing so again. Another square of paper lay on top of the podium, its surface adorned with an interior in the style of Basista. He wasn't inclined to examine the details. To do so, he felt, would profane his experience.

He turned his thoughts to the task that lay before him. That he would still make every effort to deliver his message was hardly in question. The prospect of abandoning his mission at this point was scarcely thinkable. While the woman that he sought unleashed the vengeance of the scourge in an impossible landscape that he could scarcely fathom, he was reasonably certain that she resided in the flesh somewhere on the upper floor of this apartment. Whatever services he might receive in exchange for his delivery were bound to be more merciful that those administered to the high-ranking official.

He paused to construct a mental map of the apartment, so far as he was familiar with it. Though he'd encountered very little of its sizable interior, the building's layout unfolded in his mind as if he were looking at a blueprint. The topology seemed intangibly connected to that of the House of Abnegation. Each was arranged in accordance with a single, basic principle. Duly prepared to make his way like a thief through the corridors and chambers before him, he slipped through one of the double doors and back into the office.

What little light was afforded the space came from a single bulb out in the hall. The house lamps had been dimmed for the night to an exquisite, tawny glow. The flame-tinged shadows enshrouded him as he stepped into the corridor, the soft illumination falling over his shoulders like the mantle of a man of prestige. He felt as if he now belonged in the apartment. The surrounding aesthetic seemed almost to embrace him. He wondered if Jadwiga, in a blatant act of disobedience, had provided him with a key. Her litany had done anything but drive him out. He scarcely felt more welcome in his own tiny home.

Florian crept down the hall and around the bend, his footsteps falling like flower petals on tiles of precious ivory. He ascended a stairway and proceeded toward his goal with the familiarity of a long-standing servant. He could sense Mirosław's bedroom passing under his feet and the maid's own unremarkable quarters down on the ground floor. Though he was certain that he knew precisely where it was, the notion of Telesfora's room was like a blank spot in his mental map. His attempts to envision the sizable chamber produced little more than a crystalline void. It felt as if he were grasping at ice.

The entrance to the chamber lay atop another half-stair. The dark, polished wood was covered with a strip of carpet adorned with traceries and lattices of pale cream and crimson. No title announced the dwelling place of the mistress of the house. One might mistake it for the entrance to a storage closet, save for its prominent location. The flower in its metal ball emitted an audible hum as he approached the modest door. It thirsted for its recipient like an addict waiting for a fix. Without pausing to knock, Florian passed through the entrance, only vaguely surprised to find it unlocked. His heart sank in his chest as he stepped into a chamber abandoned by its occupant.

In the center of the room was an opulent bed with a headboard of finely carved oak. The elaborations of the frame reached nearly to the ceiling, its shadows cast in multiple directions by a variety of hanging lamps. An unpretentious bedsheet of charcoal and deep burgundy had been hastily pulled back. The recent presence of the sought-after woman still reverberated through the unoccupied space. A quick glance around the perimeter of the chamber revealed no trace of the escapee. Given the extravagance of the furnishings, it was beyond question that he'd come to the right place.

Niches circled the perimeter of the room, their hollows containing the well-preserved heads of spotted leopards and gazelles, among a host of other beasts. Their gazes were turned without exception to the vacated bed in the center of the room. The shadows of their profiles were projected onto the floor by the flames of candelabras set into the plaster above them. They looked like nothing so much as a council of ministers enwrapped in contemplation of the royal throne.

Below the high niches hung a series of silken banners. Their dimensions and coloring, along with the images on their surfaces, bore a striking similarity to the one found in the assembly room. These were arranged according to the contrast in colors between their backgrounds and designs, proceeding in chromatic order from one side to the other. Each of them depicted a house of influence of its own, its exterior shown amidst a natural calamity that seemed to exemplify its nature. Some were erected amidst surging waves or perched on perilous crags while others were menaced by raging infernos to which they seemed to be impervious. The intimate depths of their interiors were revealed in the shimmering lines that graced their surfaces. Florian took care not to lose himself in their circuitous elaborations.

He allowed himself only the briefest survey of the range of banners that hung nearest him. Just as with the depiction of the House of Abnegation, a recurring cast of characters could be discerned behind their walls. He noted thieves and seducers, sycophants and saboteurs, along with an inscrutable machine housed in an upper chamber of each of them. An anomalous matriarch moved through the houses as well, her appearance, actions, and manner of dress slightly differing from one to another. He found no trace of his own figure among the intrigues of the inhabitants. He could sense that he was forbidden to set foot inside these houses. Why he'd been allowed to do so even once was a mystery. He could only suppose that Kazimira's message had given him special dispensation.

One of the banners was conspicuously missing. A notable gap was found between indigo and teal. In its place appeared an open window affording a spectacular view of the rooftops of the city. It was evidently here that Telesfora had absconded. Florian stepped over to the window and placed his hands upon the sill, leaning his head out into the cool night air. The streetlamps below stood like inconsolable vassals that had been abandoned by their liege. Not a single living soul could be seen among them. It seemed likely that Telesfora had left only a few minutes before. She would be clever enough to escape the eyes of the onlooker from above.

Florian was confident that she'd managed the descent without falling to her death. Whether she'd scaled the outer walls or used some other means of escape remained an open question. While he'd lost her for the time being, he had no doubt that his task would continue until the message was delivered. The urgency of his assignment rang through him like a call to battle. He would pursue her to the ends of the earth if need be, leaving the shell of his life behind him. If his pursuit were to consume the remainder of his days, he would not have lived in vain.

An Incident in the House of Destiny

The Argument

"THE destiny of humanity, if such a thing can be said to exist," said Ferdinand, "is driven by nothing more profound than trial and error." He gripped the stem of the hookah with the fingers of an eager hand and filled his mouth with a rich burst of tobacco. He looked nothing short of stunning in his dark gray, tailored suit. He had always been a handsome man. His penchant for fine clothing complimented his naturally delicate features, the gentle slope of his brow, the congeniality of his soft blue eyes.

Oscar, for his part, was dressed in a tasteful ensemble of fine, blue silk. The tight fit of his smoking robe betrayed a slightly underdeveloped physique. "The trouble with you is that you have the soul of a pragmatist," he said, two fingers raised to his lower lip. "The rational mind is your god, king, and priest. You gaze upon the world through its inadequate lens and you're blind to anything that falls outside its view."

"It just so happens that your god is a poet and mine a proper mathematician," insisted Ferdinand, letting the soporific effect of the tobacco sooth his every nerve. "Your faith seeks to reinvent the world according to an exalted ideal, while mine is content to reveal the world exactly as it is."

The sitting room of Oscar's apartment was arranged with the precision of a finely-cut jewel. The two men sat on leather armchairs before a black lacquer table. An oversized window afforded a spectacular view of the city as it ceded to the embraces of sunset. The lengthening shadows bathed a motley array of tenement buildings in pale shades of indigo and mauve while the defiant steeple of a nearby church emerged in triumph from their midst.

"You admit to the validity of esoteric forces and the faculty of second sight, yet you deny their connotations," said Oscar as he grasped the second stem of the hookah from its resting place. "Your views are inconsistent. Your theory and your practice disagree with one another. One is led to the conclusion that your argument is disingenuous." He stuck the pipe in his mouth and gently sucked, summoning the smoke as if it were an elemental spirit.

"Not in the least," insisted Ferdinand. "Nature's hidden forces are entirely blind and have no more meaning than the pull of gravity. As for the visions of the clairvoyant, these are nothing more than phantoms in the mirror of their own unconscious. The existence of the soul is a poetic delusion. We're intelligent animals and nothing more. I haven't a single reason to believe that the machinery of the universe operates according to anything but a fixed set of mechanical laws."

"Of course, we can debate the matter as much as you like," said Oscar. "Neither of us will ever be convinced as to the other's point of view. What I propose is this: let us find out for certain."

"And how might you suggest we do that?" asked Ferdinand.

"I think I have just the thing." Oscar rose from his chair and stepped over to one of the bookshelves. After a quick scan of the spines he pulled a thick volume from a high shelf, brought it over to the table, and placed it down before his friend.

The book, bound in luxuriant, black leather, featured an image pressed in gold leaf on the front—an upraised hand with the outermost fingers slightly flexed, in the palm of which appeared a flaming triangle. No title was displayed on either the cover or the spine, yet Ferdinand could hardly fail to recognize the tome. It was a fairly recent edition of *The Book of the Night Goat* put out by a local publisher. It had initially surfaced several centuries before among a disaffected circle of aristocrats. It appeared to be a mystical treatise, if a heretical one at the very least—pious supplications had been interspersed with the basest of obscenities, all peppered with perplexing riddles and cryptographic tables. The book was met with nearly universal condemnation when it had first appeared, though it had recently enjoyed something of a resurgence in the occult small press.

Oscar opened the cover and carefully flipped through the pages. A number of extravagant images went by, their symbolic connotations so impossibly arcane that the artistry itself was overshadowed. Naked celebrants clasped blades or torches in their hands while their eyes were bound with blindfolds and their feet surrounded by flaming candles. They stood within circles and other geometric forms whose boundaries were circumscribed with impenetrable formulae. Oscar's fingers came to a resting point roughly midway through the book. The two pages on display were filled with tables of holy names whose letters had been permuted according to particular rules. He pointed to a sequence that was preceded by a header in decorative, scarlet text: "To gain knowledge of destiny, of the unfolding of first causes, and of the means by which all things arise from the will of the creator."

"I take it you're quite serious?" said Ferdinand without looking up, his fingers tightening their grip on the stem of the hookah.

"I can't think of a single reason why I wouldn't be," said Oscar. "After all, we're both experienced occultists. There's nothing to prevent us from opening the gates to the visionary world this very evening. I have in mind an opening ritual that I believe will serve our purpose."

Ferdinand considered the prospect. He had to admit that the formulae found within the pages of the book had made him curious. Both Oscar and himself had spent considerable time rising through the ranks of the prominent occult lodges of the day. They'd mastered the rites of multiple systems, amassed a formidable vocabulary of esoteric terms, and made the elemental forces and the inner planes their playthings. Ferdinand had approached the work from a purely psychological angle, yet he'd found it useful and had kept up his practices over the years. He could think of a thousand reasons to abstain from the experiment that Oscar was proposing, yet his interest had been piqued and in the end he agreed.

"Excellent. We're all set, then." Oscar lifted the book with care, still open, from the table. "Of course, you being the skeptic in this case, it's only fitting that you should be the one to receive the vision. If all goes well, the truths perceived will leave a profound impression on your soul and you'll come humbly before me and admit that you've been sorely remiss."

"If such a thing occurs," remarked Ferdinand, "I should be more than happy to do so."

The Bureaucrat

Théophile passed through a serpentine maze of narrow byways and expansive boulevards on his way to the administrative district. The glaring light of countless streetlamps suffused the city in an overwhelming glow, nearly blotting out the luminescence of the stars. Taxicabs hobbled at precarious speeds along the uneven, cobblestone roads while trolleys packed with evening revelers glided along a crisscrossing network of rails. One thousand nameless faces paraded up and down the city streets, each one of them complicit in the stratagems of history. The night embraced them all with the same casual indifference as if not a single one among them was distinguishable from the others.

The imposing façade of the National Assembly Building stood along the western rim of Imperial Square. Constructed several centuries past, it still retained an undeniable dignity, a loftiness which gently ennobled those who stood beneath its shadow. Eight tall pillars flanked the main entrance, while a lofty pediment above displayed an allegorical tableau. The north and south arms of the building extended to the further extremes of the square, their rooftops lined with statues depicting the ancient gods of law and commerce. Like a luminous palace it shone beneath the pale sky, eagerly proclaiming its authority to the populace it served.

Théophile ascended the wide staircase before the main entrance to the building. He was met by a senior officer of the gendarmerie, himself supported by two customary officers that stood to either side of the imposing doorway. They dignified the night with their dark blue tunics, gold epaulettes, and black shakos. Théophile dutifully produced the necessary papers, though the officers knew him well.

"Does the magistrate of midnight oil return so soon?" quipped the senior gendarme, his arms clasped behind his back. "I would have thought you'd routed every inquiry in the house by now."

"Alas, the work of a minor official is never finished," said Théophile as he replaced his papers in an inner pocket of his jacket. "Walk with me, Gaspard. I would converse with you a little before submitting to the tedium of my administrative duties."

"I cannot think of a single thing that I would more desire, " said the senior gendarme, confident that his supporting officers would maintain order in his absence.

The two men set out along their usual route, taking them around the perimeter of the building. They walked in silence for a moment as Théophile lit a cigarette. He offered the open pack to his companion, knowing full well that his offer would be refused. "Never on duty, as you know."

Théophile pointed with his cigarette to the hazy, washed-out splendor of the night sky above them. "Behold, the aristocracy of heaven," he observed. "I once thought that the stars themselves comprised the true nobility, but now I look above me and see little more than a vast bureaucracy. I feel certain that the constellations are as hopelessly labyrinthine as our own ignoble institutions. They mock us in their impenetrability. How many millions of them swarm above us, each one perfectly maintaining its essential function in the grand tapestry of human destiny, inspiring us to build great empires only to watch them crumble into dust?"

"I wouldn't know," replied the senior gendarme. "I can scarcely see a single star through the glow of the city lights."

Théophile tapped his cigarette, sending tiny flakes of smoldering ash down to the cold concrete at his feet. "You play the part of the realist with admirable aplomb," said he.

"I come from a long line of realists," replied the senior gendarme. "One might say that it's my destiny to uphold the tradition."

"One might say so," replied Théophile. "One might respond that there are only two traditions extant, of which all others are merely types. One tradition serves the reign of quality, while the other serves the reign of quantity. I recently came across the idea in an obscure little book containing the memoirs of a French civil servant from a couple decades past. A bitter little man was he. Perhaps more so even than myself. Upon reading, I was struck with the notion that, while I strive to serve the one, I inevitably end up playing into the hands of the other. You, on the other hand, would be perfectly happy to uphold the tenets of either, yet still you somehow manage to bring something of quality to the world."

"I serve the reign of the sensible," insisted the senior gendarme, the very image of decorum beneath the red plume of his shako. "Which, I am quite certain, is perfectly agnostic to all such distinctions."

Théophile, having nothing more to say, placed his cigarette between his lips and continued in silence. The pair passed east by north, making their way around to the back of the building. They strolled beneath lithe branches stripped bare by winter's auspices. The trunks from which they sprouted were lined up in a perfect row before the wide boulevard that spanned the building's posterior. Théophile's cigarette had exhausted itself by the time they'd come around again to the main entrance. He tossed it gently to the ground and turned to face his friend.

"I confess," he said. "I'm not yet ready to resign myself to the ocean of paperwork that awaits me. If you would consent to undertake with me a brief stroll through our hall, I would remain forever in your debt."

164

"I could not refuse such a request even if I wanted to," said the senior gendarme with genuine warmth. They stepped inside the wide front door and into the spacious main hall. Two broad stairways led up to the assembly chambers and to the several small administrative offices that surrounded them. In the center of the expanse between them towered a noble figure carved in rich, veined marble.

Robed, winged, and graced with insupportable dignity, the statue imparted a magnificence that took Théophile's breath away. One hand held a flaming lamp while the other was raised, palm forward, in a gesture of benevolent dispensation. A woman's face gazed upward toward the mural painted onto the ceiling, her pleading eyes aggrandizing the dust itself. Seven ivory lamps were arranged in a circle around the statue's base, each burning with a finely-sculpted flame. Each of them was labeled with one of seven key principles common to architecture and government alike: Service, Truth, Authority, Harmony, Obedience, Memory, and Destiny. Théophile briefly bowed his head in recognition of his obligation to everything the figure represented.

Moving on, the pair advanced up one of the stairways and into a lofty hall. The wide corridor was lined with stately columns crowned with golden capitols, on top of which rested the lower edges of a peaked glass ceiling. The soft glow of muted starlight could just be discerned through the panes above. At the end of the hall stood an iron door while several smaller doors appeared between the rising columns. To the right lay the House of Nobility and to the left the House of Deputies.

165

Théophile ran the fingers of one hand along the surfaces of the columns as they strolled up one side of the hall and back down the other. "Touch the stones with me, Gaspard," he said. "Our building, at least, is endowed with true wisdom. Architectural truth ought to be experienced through the body as well as with the mind. Did you know that our pillars are arranged according to precise formulas and ratios? As with every aspect of this hall, they're built in accordance with our guiding principles."

The senior gendarme declined to raise a hand to sample the rough texture. "I remember hearing something to that effect during my initial orientation," he remarked. "From what I gather, it's intended to produce a pleasing effect on the eye."

"On the soul, Gaspard, on the soul!" Théophile turned from his examination of one of the crowns. "We must strive to be more than mere aesthetes. Beauty is nothing more than a side effect of truth."

"A mnemonic for the soul then, if you like," the senior gendarme commented. "Though I would call into question your notion of truth. My occupation seldom allows time for any such considerations. What appears to be true in the moment must be made to suffice."

"Alas," said Théophile with a hint of resignation. "The same is all too true for all of us. I'd like to believe the flame of tradition still burns within my heart, but I'm afraid the waters of due process have long since extinguished the torch. I suspect I'm of an accursed lineage—we aim for the eternal only to make a dismal mess of the temporal. My aspiration has remained intact, though I've largely lost track of what I'm supposed to aspire to. To judge from my work, I exist to facilitate an endless succession of minor partisan concerns. Still, I feel I must desperately cling to the higher ideals that guide me. However hopeless my efforts might turn out to be in practice, I would sup at the table of the elect and drink the wine of the sublime."

"Well, if those so noble as to procure it might be so kind as to bring me back a scrap or two, I'd be curious to try their exalted cuisine," replied the senior gendarme. "In the meantime, I'm more than content to drink the lowly wine my father drank, and his father before him. I'm descended not only from sensible realists, but from civil servants. We take our pleasure not in the eternal, but in service to the common. There's a flame that burns within our hearts as well. It is a human flame, and it's good enough for us. In point of fact, our tradition holds that it's the only flame that burns at all."

"I envy your tradition with whatever animated cobweb dust remains in my emaciated heart," said Théophile. "I remain convinced that you're an earthly saint, and on that sad day when your breath expires, all good things will perish with it."

"And you, my friend," the senior gendarme bowed, "are among the finest that the world of minor official-dom has to offer, whether or not you ever come to accept as much."

Each proceeded on their way, the senior gendarme back to his station before the main entrance of the building and Théophile to a tiny office in an upper level of the complex. A pristine arrangement lay before him as he flicked on the overhead light. Compact, organized, and doggedly efficient, his workplace was designed to represent the structure of the building in miniature. Reams of paper, neatly bundled and stacked, lined the wall beneath the window while a small library of reference volumes occupied a meager bookshelf behind polished glass doors. The tiny window afforded a limited view of Imperial Square bathed in the electric light of the streetlamps. Thèophile sat himself in a little chair before his desk and applied himself with diligence to another night's work.

The Anarchist

A silver disk sat upon a tea tray covered in rich silks of scarlet and deep blue. Natalia sat behind the makeshift altar, head bowed, eyes half-open, feet neatly tucked beneath her legs. A woman of elegance and refinement, slender yet far from slight, her dainty form was cradled by a rolling stream of incense smoke. The tiny attic room was filled with its inviolable scent as stones of myrrh and copal smoldered in a copper bowl before her. The moon, nearly full, gushed with light like holy blood from behind its partial covering of cloud, palpably shedding its influence through the tall glass windows and onto the disc's reflective surface.

Anton crouched on the other side of the altar, a ceremonial dagger clasped in one hand, his thumb pressed firmly against the cross-hilt while two primary fingers were directed down the length of the blade. He traced

168

a series of geometrical figures over the face of the silver disc, each punctuated by a short, sharp wrap of his partner's knuckles on the wooden floor.

In her mind's eye, Natalia's body was filled with a bright scarlet radiance. She lifted her head and held her palms upraised before her, passing the names of angels between her lips. She called them into the vessel of her body as if it were a church, their fiery faces glowing like a host of flaming lamps above the pulpit. Between each utterance, Anton traced a cross in the air before her.

Natalia picked up an ink brush which lay upon the altar. Petite, slender, worn, and black, it had served her more times than she could remember. It felt so comfortable in her hand that it could almost be a part of her. Dipping the brush in a thimble filled with vivid scarlet ink, she let the elemental forces travel down the conduit of her arm. The secret fire passed through her fingers and into the brush itself. Thus armed, she set about the task before her, painting, on the face of the disc, a rough yet well-executed image depicting a winged rat clutching a serpent in each paw. She worked with meticulous care, switching back and forth between the exalted heights of ecstasy and the attention to detail required of her craft. She'd performed this type of operation so many times before that she could almost do it in her sleep.

When the talisman was complete she wrapped it in black silk. Anton helped her seal the space and together they recited the closing benedictions. The ritual implements were put into their box and returned to their place in the back of a closet. They opened the windows just enough to allow the smoke of the incense to diffuse. A light drizzle drifted gently down beneath a canopy of clouds outside. The ritualists let themselves unwind for a few moments before Natalia headed out again.

"The angels of the thirteenth house have never failed me," she said as she sat directly on the floorboards. "I expect we'll see results before the week is through."

"I have not a shadow of a doubt," said Anton from his tiny bench before one of the tall windows. He rested his elbow on the windowsill while his fist supported his bearded chin. "The momentum of destiny stands behind us."

"Destiny, nothing," Natalia remarked as she poured herself a glass of brandy. "The aristocracy can't help but pitch themselves into blunder after blunder with or without our help. A little shove will merely serve to expedite the inevitable. A scandal will ensue, a shadow will be cast over the House of Nobility, and many an official in high standing will fall into disgrace."

"A short, sharp push to the left is what I have in mind," said Anton.

"A handful of the nobility will topple like dominoes, one after the other. It will be quite a delicious little spectacle. You'll see." Natalia dipped a finger into her brandy, raised it to her lips, and licked the fiery nectar directly from her skin.

Anton looked out of the window, tracking the comings and goings of the people on the streets below. His clothes had been carefully chosen so as to comprise a sort of uniform—brass buttons, polished boots, an assortment of martial caps. He cut his beard in a variety of styles resembling that of the nobility of previous centuries. He fancied himself the herald of a latent society, an affectation for which Natalia teased him mercilessly at every possible opportunity.

The apartment in which they lived was located on the outskirts of the business district. The building had been standing for several centuries. It had been built in a style which was once considered classic, but which had long since fallen out of favor. The space was cramped and chilled in the winter, and Anton and Natalia kept it sparsely decorated, yet the bare wood had its particular charm and the lack of space kept it cozy enough. Plaster busts of Novalis and Schiller sat on the tops of two low bookshelves. Anton had found them at a second-hand shop a couple of years before and had bought them without the slightest idea who they were.

"Your father," he began, looking over to Natalia with a hint of uncertainty on his face.

"My father won't suffer." Natalia reclined against a pillow. "There's money enough in the family to keep us going for another seven generations, if not twice that. All he stands to lose is a little dignity and power, which he's never had the wit to put to proper use."

"Respectfully, my dear, I cannot agree," Anton raised his chin a little. "Your father is a man of wit, if not of wisdom. He certainly has the best of intentions. He may well be the last honest dignitary in the House."

"Oh, don't you go defending him!" Natalia shot back. "He's never done a single thing of merit. Certainly nothing deserving of his fancy title. Besides, he was an abysmal parent. He hasn't an ounce of warmth about him. He's the very picture of an aristocrat—without soul, heart, conscience, or purpose."

"I'm well aware of how you feel about the man," said Anton, clasping his hands on the lapels of his military tunic. "There's no question that he adheres to an obsolete ethic. The structural foundations of the nobility have rotted from the inside out. Having no center, they cling to the façade of an edifice that no longer serves them. They can't but fall."

"I can't but push," shrugged Natalia, draining the last dregs from her glass.

Natalia's lack of sentiment for her father grated on Anton. While he loathed the institution that the man represented, he couldn't help but admire his character. At the hidden heart of his own ideology lay a veneration of traditional values, though he fervently denied the principle of the nobility of blood. On the other hand, he secretly romanticized a notion that was not dissimilar—that of the passing of the torch of virtue from one hand to another to preserve the ideals of a distant past. As much as he resented his esteem for the aristocracy, he was unable to deny, if he was honest with himself, that he desperately wanted to be one of them.

Natalia, on the other hand, was simply bored to tears with the upper class. She'd been bred nearly to death with every expectation that she would rise to prominence within the ranks of the elect, yet the opportunities afforded to her gender were ornamental at best and her natural proclivities were frowned upon. She'd felt estranged from both her parents from an early age, as they from her. It was clear that she in no way belonged to their elite society. They tried their very best to accept her as she was, but they simply didn't have it in them. When she'd come of age, she'd taken pains to dissociate herself from her family, intentionally causing a tumultuous scene in full view of several well-chosen witnesses. She still maintained a tenuous connection to her father's office, though all expectations of a rise to prominence had been lifted from her shoulders. From that point on, she was able to live quite comfortably on the modest monthly stipend deposited into an account kept open for her at the national bank.

"Monarchy and aristocracy have had their day," said Anton. "Democracy, too, will reveal itself in the light of its own iniquity. For now, we'll allow the left to thrive while the right plummets to its death. This will bring us one step closer to the true society. The key to the kingdom, so coveted by the nobility, has shattered in their very midst. Each of us bears a fragment, whether we know it or not. It's the common man who is the true heir to the sacred relics of the ancients, and the god within which will administer the sacraments. The new society will quietly assume its natural authority while the wheels of governance slowly grind themselves to nothing."

"You are insufferable," droned Natalia. "You naïve mystification of anarchist rhetoric doesn't impress me in the least. Democracy is a sham, I'll give you that, and the monarchy is little more than a long-running joke, but the many have always been ruled by the few and will continue to be so whether it's done openly or otherwise. The houses of the aristocracy need a good shaking up, is all. They grow stagnant, the elect. They need to be reminded on occasion that they've become intoxicated by their own self-importance."

With that, she picked up the talisman, concealed in its layer of silk, and placed it into one of the compartments of her shoulder bag. "Our talisman will hang from one of the statues at the back of the House of Nobility. I haven't yet decided which. I'll be back within the hour, most likely. Don't wait up for me." With her bag flung over one shoulder, she headed out into the night.

The Vision

Ivory candles in chamber sticks of gold were placed on painted sigils around the perimeter of the circle, their flames rising like cherubim through the high winds of the Empyrean. Their light shone with a penetrating glow through the billowing clouds of incense smoke that suffused the intimate bounds of the circle. Oscar dolefully intoned a holy litany, his voice rising in both pitch and vigor as he approached the climax of the invocation. The skirts of cryptographic angels swept unseen above their heads from one end of the room to the other.

Ferdinand sat kneeling in the center of the circle, the portals of his senses firmly sealed. He quietly recited the barbarous names until they rang like peals of thunder through the subtle airs. Upward he rose on invisible currents, leaving the physical confines of his body far behind him. Stripped of his outer vestments, he ascended without effort like a mustard seed borne up by an ocean.

He rose through glorious vistas of mystical vision which he abandoned one by one for ever more exalted heights. Through jeweled halls and starlit palaces he passed with little effort, forsaking their allure with an almost puritanical stoicism. He was determined to pierce the vault of the heavens that the mysteries he sought may reveal themselves in full. He burst through veils of increasing subtlety until he stood at last before an image of a heavenly woman crowned with sapphire.

Infallibly blessed by the celestial hosts was she—one hand holding a flaming beacon and the other raised in a sign of benediction. Her robe billowed with the breath of the immortal beloved while her wingtips scraped the foot of the throne. Her gaze was kept upward, lest her countenance overwhelm the weary pilgrim, while the names of ancient kings blazed in a circle at her feet. Scarcely had Ferdinand laid eyes upon her stunning beauty than was he raised, as if by winds sublime, into a hall of fiery pillars.

The flaming capstones atop the columns cast vibrant shadows on the ivory below. Each of them was inscribed in gold with a letter in an unknown tongue. Veils were stretched between them, concealing the entrances to the chambers of the just. On the left lay the House of Destiny and on the right the House of Chance. Between them, in terms at once transparent and obscure, the mandates of Heaven were inscribed onto tablets of diamond. The decrees combined the royal with the sacerdotal, impressing the laws of priest and king alike onto the soul of the world.

Ferdinand caught sight of a flurry of motion to his left. A figure emerged from the shadows behind one of the pillars—a woman enwrapped in long, dark robes, her face obscured by a halo of mist. She disappeared without a sound through one of the veils. Without giving it a second thought, he didn't hesitate to follow her as she proceeded into the House of Destiny.

The hallowed hall was nearly overwhelming in its splendor. Majestic rays of sunlight shone through the brightly-colored glass of a row of tall, arched windows that lined the far wall. Before them stood thrones of immaculate coral lined with winding veins of sapphire. Saintly figures carved in stone stood behind the seats of the elect, exerting their influence over their inhabitants when the chamber was in session. Several rows of benches lined with red and black velvet stood arranged in a descending series of semi-circles, all converging upon a central podium illuminated by a shaft of light.

A document sat upon the surface of the podium, an ivory parchment rolled up and bound with a thread of scarlet silk. By now, the dark woman had traversed one of the stairways and was swiftly approaching the stand. By the time she'd passed by it, the document was no longer lying on its surface. Swiftly, like a bolt of lightning, a winged figure of terrible size disengaged from one of the stained glass windows behind the thrones. A spire was thrust through the body of the thief, pinning her to the paving stones. The pilfered document fell from her lifeless fingers and rolled across the floor. The hand of vengeance withdrew from the pike, the imposing figure falling back into the colored glass as quickly as it had emerged. By the time Ferdinand had registered the act, the hall had again fallen silent. All that could be heard was the echo of a solemn chorus that wafted like a cloud of incense through the chamber.

Ferdinand remained impassive, content to watch the action unfold. He had no doubt that the ensuing revelation would continue to reveal itself according to its own particular logic. He slipped back through the portal and set out to explore the complex further. He passed through labyrinthine corridors of limestone and alabaster, willfully losing himself among the palatial architecture. Plaques of gold and silver engraved with official sounding titles were affixed to massive columns placed unevenly throughout the halls. One of them in particular caught his eye: *Bureau of Causality and Temporal Affairs*. Without delay, he headed toward the office indicated by the sign.

He passed through a grand archway into a modest chamber. A single desk of onyx sat in the center of a marble floor beneath a glorious arrangement of flaming lamps. On the far side of the desk sat an official-looking man dressed in the impeccable uniform of a civil servant. He clasped an ink pen in one hand, which he held suspended above a document. He gazed into the depths of the printed page as if lost in the labyrinth of fine, black script. Swiftly and without movement of the feet, Ferdinand took himself to a slender bench before the desk. The man looked up from his work with fastidious eyes, his gaze falling upon Ferdinand like a concentrated ray of piety. Without so much as a single word, he invited his guest to state his business.

"I'd like to report an incident in the House of Destiny," said Ferdinand, slightly awed by the stature of the entity before him.

"Of course," said the official. "I'm more than happy to serve you." The polished brass buttons of his uniform glowed beneath the flames of the lamps above. "What is it precisely that took place?"

"A document was stolen and the theft was avenged," replied Ferdinand.

"Very well," said the man, nonplussed. "An act of vengeance in the House of Destiny. Can I presume that the thief has been disposed of?"

"That is correct," said Ferdinand.

"Were you a witness to the scene?" he asked.

"I was," affirmed the visionary.

"And there were no other witnesses?"

"None that I know of," said Ferdinand.

"So," the man put down his pen and folded his milk-white hands before him. "You are complicit in the act."

Ferdinand paused, hesitant to contradict his host. "I'm not entirely certain that I understand," he said at last.

"It's easy to explain," said the official. "Your fate is all tied up with the event. It's become a part of you. The perpetrator of a crime and the witness of the same are bound to one another as if by an invisible contract. Theft, vengeance—these are universal themes. They can be traced back to some of the earliest events that transpired both in Heaven and on earth. Now, let me ask you this—were you seen by either the thief or the thief's assailant?"

Ferdinand thought back. He certainly didn't recall being apprehended by the dark woman, nor by the avenging angel. Scarcely had he stepped through the veil and into the chamber than did the drama unfold before him. "No," he said. "No, I don't think I was."

"And do you know the identity of the thief or the motive for the theft?" The official's expression was a mask of patience and sagacity.

"I haven't a clue as to either of these things," confirmed Ferdinand.

The heavenly figure leaned back in his chair. "Ah, now, you see?" he said. "The thief harbors a secret and now you have one as well. It's as if you stand on two sides of a mirror. And yet, each of you being blinded by your own reflection, neither of you can see the face of the other. It makes no difference that the thief has been slain—the act itself is timeless. As for the punishment, well ... one takes on something of the burden of the executioner when one is party to an execution. Now perhaps do you begin to understand the complicity you share?"

"I suppose I do," said Ferdinand, no wiser than before. "Yet I don't quite see what bearing this has on the theft of the document."

"It's a small matter," said the official with an understated flourish of the hand. "The implications of what I've said will play out in their own way. We can no more control this than can a sail control the wind. In any case, there's little for us to do in that regard. There are other matters that require our attention." He put the document before him to one side, reached into a drawer of the desk, and pulled out a fresh form. He filled out a few blank boxes before continuing.

"The theft and its punishment took place in the House of Destiny, you say." He turned his attention back to Ferdinand. "It would seem reasonable to conclude that this was destined to occur, but of course it's not so easy as that. If it was simply a matter of destiny, why didn't the officials who serve in the chamber foresee it and prevent it from happening in the first place? Or, perhaps they did have foreknowledge and allowed it to take place for some reason that remains unknown to us. Perhaps this, too, was written in the stars. We'll need a statement from each of the presiding Lords, along with those of the House of Chance. We'll take an official statement from yourself as well. The relative merits of each point of view must then be weighed, combined, refined, and permuted until we've arrived at the irreducible truth of the matter. Only then will it be possible to act in strict accordance with both natural and cosmic law. Now then." The man rose from the desk, having filled out the remainder of the form as he explained the matter. "Let us proceed with all due haste. There is much work to be done."

Catastrophe

The expansive boulevards of the administrative district looked deserted and forsaken in the stillness of the winter night. The pavement was still slick with rain, though the downpour had ceased for the time being.

The blazing light of streetlamps shone like the seditious fires of an army in revolt. Natalia stepped gingerly from city square to narrow thoroughfare, clutching the handbag that concealed the fateful disc of silver. The city embraced her like a comrade in arms, her quarrelsome nature complementing its own tumultuous history.

In the daytime, she was recognized by the occasional passerby. Her photograph had appeared in the local papers several times in recent years. Most often, her depictions in the press were limited to the idle speculations of the gossip columnists. Her periodic breaches of acceptable conduct pleased their vitriolic pens, though it was generally acknowledged that her public outbursts were of little real consequence. The truth was that she enjoyed straddling the line between unimportance and notoriety.

Coming at last to her destination, Natalia crossed the lonely expanse of Imperial Square and scampered up the concrete steps to the main entrance of the National Assembly Building. A glint of recognition appeared on the face of the gendarme who awaited her at the door. Natalia had spoken with him several times before, though she could never quite recall his name. He bowed low before her, the golden tassels on his epaulettes swinging forward with the sweep of his torso. "Her honorable disgrace, the princess heretic of black sheep," he exclaimed, eyes closed with one hand extended in greeting. "To what may I credit the honor of your presence at our venerable place of governance?"

"I've come to destabilize the markets and devalue the national currency," she said, vaguely waving her identity papers in the air before her. "While I'm here I suppose I'd better drop off some documents for my father."

"Without a doubt, without a doubt." The dignified man rose again. "You may leave the papers with me or take them up yourself. Perhaps you'd wish to cause a scandal in the House of Deputies as well?"

"I hadn't thought of it." Natalia stepped through the door which had been opened for her, momentarily resting a hand upon the shoulder of one of the lesser officers as she passed. "I suppose it would only be fair, given the trouble I've managed to stir up for the nobility. I'll see what I can do."

"I tremble inwardly to think, my enfant terrible, of precisely what you may be capable." He waved Natalia through the door as if she hadn't already taken the liberty.

"I'll do my utmost not to let you down," said Natalia over her shoulder as she headed for the stairs. "In any case, I'll be out of your hair in no more than a minute or two." She'd been running errands for her father for so long that her presence in the building was no cause for concern. She'd made a minimal effort over the years to keep the gendarmes familiar with her face. It seemed a simple matter of strategy to ensure that she could slip in and out of the building anytime she pleased.

She had no intention of stopping by her father's office, heading instead, along a circuitous route, to the chamber of the House of Nobility. She would only need a minute inside of the hall to put the talisman in place behind one of the statues. She couldn't be bothered with an excess of caution. There was little chance that she'd be apprehended in the act and the consequences would be minor if she was.

She passed between the pillars in the central hallway and opened one of the doors. She made use of a key which had been pilfered from her father several months earlier. The front end of the chamber was awash with golden light, with its stained glass windows, podium, and statues. The hall's interior served as an unwelcome reminder of the expectations that had been placed upon her from the time that she was young. She was burdened with four brothers, every one of which had assumed a role within the ranks of civil service. They'd been taught to make a lifestyle out of doing as little as possible. Their modus operandi was to preserve rather than to create. It had been a maxim in her family that the highest possible honor lay in the maintenance of a flame that had been kindled long ago, and by inference it was accepted that none of them had any business lighting fires of their own. This was simply not compatible with Natalia's inclinations. While it was not her intention to set the world aflame, she had an insatiable appetite for scandal. She was content to strike the occasional match to provide a much-needed luster to a slowly rotting carcass that had once shown signs of life.

Natalia passed into the hallowed hall where once the sacerdotal authorities announced the judgments of Heaven. She'd barely stepped over the threshold before she caught sight of a horrific scene. A chandelier of impressive size lay on the podium in the center of the hall. It must have fallen from the ceiling—she hadn't noticed it when she'd first come in. The surrounding area was littered with broken glass, while the podium itself was drenched in dark black blood. Her father lay in the embrace of a young woman who had been relieved of all her clothing, both of them crushed beneath the weight of the lamp that had pinned their lifeless bodies to the unyielding wood. A shaft of moonlight that shone through one of the windows illuminated the scene. The reflection of the colored light upon the scattered glass gave rise to a dazzling spectacle of iridescence.

She froze in her tracks, strangely calm in the face of such a devastating shock. An icy indifference took hold of her. She found herself wondering if it concealed an ocean of pain beneath its surface. It took her no time at all to collect herself. She knew that she must leave at once. She didn't want to be there when the authorities arrived. She couldn't bear the tedium of answering their questions. That would come later, only after the initial excitement had died down.

Already, she was scheming—how, she wondered, might she possibly explain her presence in the building? It would be abundantly clear that she'd deceived the senior gendarme at the very least. She began composing a statement that would allow her to take refuge in the inviolable sanctuary that was afforded to the well-connected. It would be best if she contacted the family lawyer. She would do so without delay. She briskly walked back through the labyrinth of corridors and down a narrow stairway that ran along the back wall of the building. The talisman was still concealed in a pocket of her shoulder bag. Any thought as to her own complicity in the incident was quickly pushed aside. She slipped out through one of the iron doors that let out to the back, passing by one of the many officers stationed about the grounds. Feeling strangely free, as one often does when confronted with the loss of something essential, and having not the slightest clue as to what direction her life might take from that point on, she surrendered to the mercy of the night, setting off on a meandering route toward her apartment.

Théophile, just moments earlier, had risen from his desk in order to refresh himself with a short stroll around the interior of the building. As he passed between the pillars on the upper floor, he couldn't help but notice that one of the doors was ajar. He paused, not entirely certain whether he should alert the gendarme. What harm, he thought, could possibly result from taking a quick look? He'd never seen either of the chambers entirely unoccupied. The thought of the assembly hall lit only by moonlight drew him eagerly toward the open door.

Enter the venerable chamber he did, and what he saw there struck his heart with such a terrible shock that he nearly lost consciousness. He had led somewhat of a cloistered life. On only one occasion had he ever been in the presence of death. Years before, on a bitter winter evening, he'd witnessed a senseless attack upon the person of a foreign dignitary by a small group of nationalists. The imperial guard lost no time at all in shooting the attackers down before they could reach their target. The dignitary emerged from the incident unscathed, but the sudden and unexpected cessation of life had deeply upset Théophile.

Harrowing as that had been, it was as nothing compared to the abomination on the podium before him. That a high-ranking official might die in such an undignified manner was simply beyond comprehension. He put the fingertips of one hand into his mouth and bit down hard with his incisors, nearly breaking the surface of the skin. He choked back a tiny sob before resolving to go down and fetch the officers that were stationed at the entrance to the building. He knew that a scandal would be unavoidable. A full investigation would be called for. Blood had spilled in the House of Nobility and the shadow it would cast would be unavoidable in the weeks to come. Putting all such considerations out of his mind, he turned around and hurried back out of the chamber.

Before he knew it, he was again in the main hall, the central statue towering above him. Without quite knowing why, he stopped and turned around. Something about the monument disturbed him. The expression on the face of the august icon suggested the cold ambivalence of a distant star. Her eyes seemed to penetrate the veils of history, revealing the outlines of an unspoken atrocity that lay hidden at the very heart of the world. Though the presence of the statue was nearly unbearable, Théophile stood transfixed. As he continued to gaze upon the veined, white marble, a triangle of flame emerged across her upraised palm.

A theater of rolling images unfolded within the boundaries of the triangle. Though the area was not a spacious one, the vision was magnified in the larger arena of Thèophile's mind. The houses of the noble were overturned by decrees at once inscrutable and absolute. Their iron walls collapsed before the mandates of Heaven, unable to bear their unfathomable weight. The wheels of governance cracked and broke beneath the strain of the imperishable stars, those sacred principles by which the vestments of the righteous are measured and defined. The pleas of the elect rose to the floor of the Empyrean before the watchful eyes of a celestial host that was too impartial or ineffable to respond to their prayers. Providence shattered the long-standing pillars of church and state alike while the soul of humanity hung helpless in the balance. Wave after wave of brutality and cruelty rolled forth from the upraised marble palm. Thèophile fell to his knees, unable to bear the unfolding revelation.

A Conclusion of Sorts

The ritual had drawn to a close, the vision had ended, the spirits were dismissed and the veil was drawn. The proper banishings and purifications had been dutifully performed. The candles were snuffed and the carpet was unrolled over the ceremonial circle that had been painted on the floor. The silken curtains were pulled back and the light of countless streetlamps again suffused the apartment. The ritualists, fatigued to the depths of their souls, relaxed in the afterglow of their mysterium opus, the quietude of night assuaging their senses like a gentle anesthetic.

Ferdinand raised a glass of brandy to his lips and took a generous sip. The scintillating liquid tempered the fire in his heart—a gentle soporific to ease him out of the visionary state. "There's one thing of which I can be absolutely certain," he noted, his glass raised before him as if to elucidate a platitude. "I'm not the slightest bit wiser now than I was before the ritual."

"I take it that you've plumbed the depths of universal understanding and that's all you have to say for yourself?" said Oscar, reclining in his armchair.

Ferdinand took another sip of brandy, letting the slight burn of the liquor remain on his palette for a moment. "I suppose it's only fitting that I give you a full account of my experience," he said at last.

"Quite," said Oscar. "Be assured that I will not let you leave my apartment until I've received as much."

"Very well," said Ferdinand, taking a moment to collect his thoughts as he ran the fingers of one hand through his thinning hair.

"I received the vision without the slightest bit of trouble," he began. "The names divine, in this particular sequence, delivered to me everything that's promised in the book. I was sent hurling through the visionary light as if shot out of a canon, the inner planes revealing themselves in all of their majestic splendor. I pushed ever onward, never content with the wondrous sights around me. I was called to a particular destination and I let nothing distract me en route. I alighted at last in a sort of governmental building between the venerable houses of Destiny and Chance."

"A propitious beginning, to be sure." Oscar poured himself a glass of brandy, held it up to the light as if to inspect it for impurities and, finding nothing out of place, indulged in a mouthful of the intoxicating nectar.

"Before any time at all had passed, I was witness to a crime," continued Ferdinand. "A document was stolen from the House of Destiny. The theft was avenged by the death of the thief. Quite naturally, I reported the incident, aided by an administrative official in one of innumerable little offices that were found within the building. Statements were collected from the representatives of the Houses of Destiny and Chance, as well as from myself. A statement was even prepared for the thief, though it was naturally left blank."

"Precisely the sort of efficiency I would expect from such a lofty office," said Oscar.

"It must be noted," said Ferdinand, "that nobody present seemed to have the slightest interest in identifying the thief. Likewise, the motive for the theft was entirely ignored. Far more attention was given to the implications of the incident. We wound up in a sort of court of cosmic justice, an administrative office of inscrutable design in which the dispensations of the hand of providence are codified and regulated. There, I beheld a process which, as I was made to understand, underlies the very causal threads that bind one moment to the next."

Oscar had meanwhile struck a match and applied it to a disc of charcoal which was then placed into the chamber of the hookah. After waving out the match and tossing it absently through the window, he refilled

Ferdinand's glass before doing the same with his own. "Do go on," he said at last as he returned to his chair.

"How can such a place be described?" Ferdinand shifted slightly in his seat, running a hand once again through his hair. "The court consisted of an infinity of faceless, nameless officials, each identical to all the others and each belonging to a different department situated within an unfathomably byzantine organization. Each department was aligned with one of the two houses—those of Destiny and Chance. They all performed their work in service to a central figure—a mysterious and enigmatic non-persona. The latter remained anonymous and appeared to be hermaphroditic. This impartial god seemed to function as a sort of oracle, a voice of prophecy by which a final verdict on any given matter might be ascertained."

Ferdinand tempered his exposition with a sip of brandy while Oscar looked on with rapt attention.

"A number of possibilities were subjected to the court," he continued. "The incident may have been predestined to occur, for instance, or the theft may simply have been a matter of impulse. A multiplicity of subtle nuances were considered in discussion among the officials. Suppose, for instance, that the theft itself was unpredictable, but yet was bound into a larger course of destiny. In this case, whatever resulted from the incident would ultimately be subsumed. And then there was the question of my part in the matter. Was I destined to witness the act, or did I arrive on the scene of the crime purely by accident? Each of these potential interpretations were debated at great length by representatives of both houses. The intricacies of cosmic law were scrutinized by a nearly endless succession of specialists. Precedents were invoked, casebooks were examined, initiatives were drafted and voted upon. On occasion, one of the latter was vetoed by a higher power while a host of special interest groups pursued their own particular agendas.

"Above it all I could but dimly discern the traces of a distant monarch from whose Ineffable Name the infinity of laws had been derived with mathematical precision. From the monarchy of Heaven has arisen a bureaucracy of unimaginable efficiency. Our own institutions are but pale imitations of this vast and inscrutable machine.

"At last, after endless deliberations, all of the dissenting voices were combined into a document by yet another branch of the court, all in meticulous accordance with an incalculable system of rules. This document was then presented to the oracle, who proceeded to reduce the whole into a single word."

Oscar reached into a tinderbox with scarcely a sound and removed a pinch of tobacco. This he dropped upon the charcoal, placed the hookah firmly between his lips, and inhaled deeply. "And that word?" he queried as the smoke rolled forth from between his immaculate jaws.

"I wish I could tell you," Ferdinand continued, brandy glass propped up on the ends of his fingers. "But alas—it was perfectly unpronounceable. The word, as it was spoken, issued forth as a white-hot mass of extremely fine substance, neither solid, liquid nor gas. I was made to understand that it would take some time to cool, but that as it did so it would crystallize in our world. Thus, presumably, it will proceed to unfold as an event having several interrelated components, each of which bears some relation, however oblique, to the incident to which I was a witness."

"I suppose it follows," said Oscar. "The inner world of the visionary and the world in which we live are inseparably bound to one another."

"They are bound together, one might say, like the two sides of a mirror," said Ferdinand. "Further, if I understand correctly, it is precisely from this event, assuming that we're able to properly identify it, that we're to discern something of the truth that underlies the enigma of chance and destiny."

Oscar sat in silent reflection for a time, considering what he'd been told. His eyes glazed over slightly as he indulged in another mouthful of tobacco. The sound of rain pouring lightly down from Heaven could just be heard as it struck the brick façade outside, a quiet cacophony rich in texture which was gently contained in the abiding silence. "It's perfectly absurd," said Oscar, after several long moments. "I don't feel that we've made the slightest bit of headway toward the resolution to our argument."

"Precisely," said Ferdinand. "Nor do I."

"Even more than that, I feel as if I've been insulted in some subtle manner but I can't quite wrap my head around exactly how."

"I'm only relating my experience," said Ferdinand beneath the dim glow of the overhead light. "You're perfectly free to make of it what you will."

Oscar stuck the mouthpiece of the hookah between his lips and sucked in silent contemplation. "I don't like it," he said after another moment's thought. "It sounds like madness to me, nothing more than an astral delusion."

"To be sure," said Ferdinand. "I cannot disagree. Perhaps the powers that be are mocking us for our impetuosity or testing us with blasphemous falsehoods. It may be that the veil was pulled back just a little, leaving much of the matter in the dark. It's not beyond the bounds of possibility that the whole thing was simply imagined on my part, though this seems unlikely given the vivacity of the vision. In any case, we have yet to see how the whole thing plays out. There remains some possibility that an event will come to pass in the coming days that will elucidate the matter further for us, though to be quite honest, I'm not particularly hopeful."

"I suppose, then, that there's nothing we can do but wait," said Oscar, not entirely resolved within himself upon the matter.

The gentle patter of the rain increased, gradually transforming into a torrential downpour which left a dazzling pattern of circular splashes upon the surface of the window. The howling of the wind bespoke inexplicable mysteries as it rushed down the near-deserted streets, revealing subtle variations upon ancient themes observed by everything that lives. It elicited, in response, a veritable symphony of creaks and groans from the surrounding buildings. Above it all, the stars abided in their immutable stations, shedding their influence upon a world unknowing or indifferent to their stratagems and machinations.

A Night of Amethyst

Lobby
Exits: north, east, south

You stand in the lobby of an institution stained with scandal and ignominy. A symmetrical group of decorative lamps hang by thick strands from the ceiling. Their bulbs are shaped like rising flames and are arranged in tight concentric circles. A slender front desk resides on the far end of the room, behind which stands a well-dressed attendant. He wields the authority of the minor official whose expertise exceeds that of their superiors. His attention is absorbed in what appears to be an open registry.

Sitting areas of no great size lie to either side of the desk. A woman reclines in an immodest position on the elegant upholstery of one of the armchairs. She wears a button-up top of vivid emerald and a skirt of pale cream. A bare foot is propped on one of the armrests while the fingers of one hand trace lazy circles on the fabric. She appears to be intolerably bored.

To the west, behind you, is the entrance to the establishment, but of course you have no intention of leaving so soon.

> examine carpet

The mandates of the night itself are enciphered in its rich designs and its golden fringes flash like filaments against the dark, wooden floors. It occurs to you that its pattern reflects every possible path that can be taken through this game.

> approach desk

"Sir?" prompts the attendant as he looks up from the registry. "If you'll be so kind as to sign in." He turns the book around to face you. A pen lies on the desk to one side.

You've managed to attract the scrutiny of the woman in the armchair. She lies just out of view, yet you can feel her gaze on the back of your neck. You're ashamed to admit it, but this pleases you a little.

> sign registry

"Thank you kindly, Mr. Morse," says the man behind the desk after you've added your name and time of arrival. "There are a few preparations that must be attended to. If you'll be seated for a moment, we'll be ready for you shortly." He executes a barely perceptible bow before making his exit through a doorway in the east.

You turn around to confront the woman that fixes you with her gaze. She glances over to the northern archway, beyond which lies a well-lit corridor that extends in both directions. Her eyes are aflame with provocation as they return to yours. She seems to be suggesting that you slip out of the lobby before the man returns.

> examine desk

I fail to see how the front desk warrants the benefit of your attention. Nevertheless, you turn around and consider its simple elegance. The woman behind you is hardly amused that you've turned your back on her. She proceeds to make a gentle hissing sound with her tongue and the roof of her mouth, her presence over-flowing with a shameless physicality that's all the more pronounced when your attention is focused elsewhere.

> search desk

With all of the discretion of a gentleman thief, you step behind the desk. You realize that the risk you're taking is nothing short of absurd. The attendant might return at any time.

A number of items of possible interest are concealed beneath the upper ledge. Stacked neatly to one side lie five plastic cassette reels, each of which is tinted with a different hue. A paper label on the outermost reel bears a single, mystifying word (*'Récit'*). There are several other things as well, including a box of matches propped up against the ledge. Lying flat on the surface is the open registry, just behind which lies a small, hand-held monocular scope.

The woman in the armchair continues to regard you like a tiger stalking its prey. You openly display your self-consciousness by refusing to look back at her.

> examine scope

An older model, to judge from its design, scarcely longer than the palm of your hand. It has the appearance of a well-crafted toy from the days in which children were given items of quality. A golden ring around the center is engraved with an intricate floral pattern. This section of the scope appears to be designed to rotate on its axis. Etched into the metal near the lens is an ambiguous title: *The Night of Disposition.*

> take scope

Your petty theft is executed with no lack of proficiency. The scope is now concealed in an inside pocket of your vest. You wonder if the woman that's watching you has noticed what you've done. You're certain that she's following your every move.

> take matches

As if compelled by an uncontrollable urge, you take the box of matches as well. It's just small enough to avoid detection.

> search registry

Am I to assume that you're looking for your own name among the previous entries? You open the cover, flip through the pages, and find it in more than one place. It would appear that this is not the first time that you've played this game.

You can't help but turn your gaze back toward the woman in the armchair. Now that she's managed to recapture your attention, she shifts her eyes once more toward the archway to the north. Though she's clearly toying with you for her own amusement, the woman's levity is infectious. You find yourself pleased at the notion of a secret game between the two of you.

On another note, your time is running out. You'd best step away from behind the desk before the attendant returns from wherever he's gone to.

> go north

In compliance with the woman's unspoken demand, you emerge from your place behind the desk and slip out of the lobby through the northern archway.

Vermilion Corridor
Exits: east, south, west

Walls of deep, warm cinnabar rise to an arch above your head, their surfaces awash in cascading shadows cast by a row of hanging lamps. A polished wooden floor extends in either direction, leading to slender doors to the east and west. Black iron panels comprise one wall, their surfaces lined with intricate openings. The stylistic crosses arranged in alternating rows bring to mind the patterns found on the screens of confessional booths. You wonder if the woman in the lobby will betray you when the front-desk man returns. You find yourself a little disappointed that she didn't come with you.

> go west

Wishing to distance yourself from the lobby as quickly as possible, you hasten down the hall and slip through the unlocked door. Upon stepping through, you close it behind you as softly as you can. You feel like a fugitive. There's no question that you'll be pursued. What's worse, if caught, you have no reasonable excuse for having wandered so far from the lobby.

Nightwatch
Exits: north, east

The walls in this chamber are of a dark-stained wood that seems to exhaust the meager light of the single hanging lamp. Narrow tables cling to the extremities of the room, their surfaces obscured beneath pale linens and white lace. Of particular note is a sizable cupboard set into the northern wall, its surface equipped with a small brass handle and a golden lock in a circular plate. Another doorway stands some distance from the cupboard, its panels awash in gentle light. The title of this room is displayed in relief on a copper plaque that hangs near the entrance.

In the center of the room, on a crimson divan, sleeps a woman that appears a little younger than yourself. Her body is draped in a dress of rich olive that leaves her shoulders bare. One arm is lazily thrown across her brow. She wears a heavy necklace of silver and faux-ruby. She's snoring so softly that the sound is barely perceptible.

> examine woman

The stones in her necklace seem indecently exposed beneath the pallid glow of the lamp. You immediately flush with guilt at the act of watching a woman sleep. The feeling is so uncomfortable that you're urged to turn your attention elsewhere.

> wake woman

You approach her with a timid step and place a cautious hand on one bare shoulder. This accomplishes little more than to cause her to shift her position. A gentle nudge brings her fully awake, her open eyes regarding you with dazed curiosity. You take a step back, relieved that she hasn't perceived you as a threat. Her gaze remains unfocused as she runs the fingers of one hand in a drowsy line along the crest of the divan. You give her a few moments to establish her bearings. There's something undeniably intimate about watching a person rouse themselves from sleep. This is all the more so when that person is a stranger and allows themselves the vulnerability.

"Am I relieved from my shift?" she asks at last, not yet ready to sit up. "Is it time already?"

> say yes

The woman stretches and yawns, the shadow of her upraised arms sweeping over the floorboards below. She uprights herself, puts her feet upon the floor, and rests her palms on the upholstery beside her. You nervously wait as she emerges from the depths of slumber. You're painfully aware that the attendant could appear at any moment.

"I must have slept for days," the woman remarks as the gentle light embraces her. "It's so hard to tell in this place." She rises from her seat with all the opiated languor of a lotus-eater. Running a ringless hand through her thick, auburn hair, she slowly makes her way to the cabinet in the north. With another yawn, she bangs a fist against the wall to one side of the knob. She repeats the gesture two times more. You cringe each time she does this. You're terrified that the noise will attract the attention of the man you hope to avoid.

> look scope

That's just the perfect course of action. Stay right where you are. The front-desk man will come for you in no time at all. In an affront to common sense, you remove the scope from your vest and raise it to your eye. As it turns out, the scope is intended to be looked not *through*, but *into*. Immediately upon doing so, you're confronted with an image as inscrutable as it is detailed. The scene is greatly magnified through an optical trick that you assume is accomplished with mirrors. The result is so vibrant and all-encompassing that the environment seems to surround you. Further, due both to the limited palette and the style of the image, it's impossible to tell whether you're looking at a photograph or a particularly well-executed painting.

An assembly of figures occupies the frame, each of them clothed in impeccable dress. They seem to be engaged in a heated round of debates, competitions, exhortations, and trysts. They carry out their activities before a row of high façades beneath the dubious auspices of a crisp winter night. The piercing glare of several ill-placed streetlamps lends the scene the appearance of a finely-cut crystal. The structure and purpose of the intemperate congress is impossible to discern. That the members are impassioned is hardly in question—they seem almost on the verge of breaking out into a riot. They argue over bundled papers, printed pamphlets, and sealed letters, among other things of a similar nature, while others are lost in explication before a doubtful and distracted audience. Unrest is rife among the assembled. Not a single soul appears untroubled or calm. Fingers extend in accusation while the accused engage in any number of evasions. Some consult the expertise of their associates. Others cower in the shadows. The crowd is split into several factions, each of which is thoroughly invested in their own suspicions, plights, and interventions.

An additional detail demands your attention. The surrounding walls, without exception, are covered in a script of exceptional size. The contrasts of the image and the abundance of shadows makes the words impossible to read. They look to have been written by a tremendous hand with notably exquisite penmanship. The characters continue unbroken over open windows and protruding balconies, blackening doorways and wrapping around drain pipes with a meticulous degree of care. The impression given is that the buildings themselves comprise the pages of a document.

Thus *The Night of Disposition*. A wave of vertigo rushes through you as you withdraw the scope from before your eye. It takes a moment for your vision to adjust to the perspective and colors of the surrounding room. No sooner have you done so than are your nerves sharply rattled by another spate of noise. It sounds like the grinding of long-unattended gears and seems to come from somewhere behind the cabinet. You slip the scope back into your vest and return your attention to the space before you.

The woman, fully awake now, reaches a hand into a pocket of her dress. She retrieves a silver key attached to a weathered, scarlet thread. She places this into the lock below the handle, turns it to one side, and pulls the door wide open. Just as she does this, a wooden carriage can be seen descending into the space beyond. You recognize the trappings of a classical dumbwaiter, if a little larger than the typical model. Two sturdy white ropes hang in the shadows before the cabinet. Somebody's clearly lowered the box into place from another floor of the building.

Without a moment's hesitation, the woman retrieves a wooden tray from the otherwise empty interior. On its surface is found a hardbound book, not entirely dissimilar in style to the registry you'd signed earlier. A fountain pen lies to one side and a bottle of ink to the other. You imagine that any number of things must be attended to before the woman's shift is done—forms must be filled out, reports completed, and the chamber prepared for her replacement, at the very least. In adherence to duty, she carries the tray over to one of the tables against the wall.

Now, I hate to rush you, but you really ought to consider moving on. The front-desk man is bound to find you here if you remain for much longer. Needless to say, if you're so unfortunate as to be caught, you'll be thrown out of the establishment and the game will end. The doorway to the north, you can't help but notice, offers a perfectly convenient escape route.

> enter dumbwaiter

I suppose this will suffice as well. You step over to the still-open cupboard and carefully climb inside of the device.

Dumbwaiter
Exits: south

As it turns out, the carriage is just large enough to support your under-developed frame. Your companion turns and watches you with great amusement as you situate yourself inside the box. A cursory snort gives way to uninhibited laughter as she supports herself with one hand on the table. You're given the impression that it had never occurred to her to try such a ludicrous trick herself.

"I suppose you'd like to go for a ride in that thing?" she asks with incredulity after her laughter subsides. "That's a novel way to get to the upper floor, I'll give you that. Shall I take you there? I can pull the ropes for you—it's not nearly so difficult as it looks."

> say yes

You wonder if she's simply playing along as she steps over to the niche. If nothing else, you can hide yourself behind the cabinet door if the attendant comes looking for you. You're pleased by the woman's intimate presence as she leans in to grab one of the ropes. Her eyes are still hazy from having recently woken. She regards you with unconcealed geniality.

"The poets upstairs will be more than happy to receive you," she says as her fingers lightly curl around the outermost rope. "They're rarely afforded visitors these days. They would never admit it, but I think they get lonely." She tightens her grip and tests the weight. You realize, with some astonishment, that she actually intends to raise the carriage.

"You'll have to get out as soon as you can once you arrive," she says. "Here, you're at the lowest point. If I let go of the rope once the box has been raised, you'll plummet right back to the bottom. The counter-weights are only designed to support so much."

With that, her fingers tighten their grasp and she hoists you directly upward. You almost wish you could remain in her company, but of course this is impossible given the circumstances. "Just bang on the cupboard door when you get there," she calls as you ascend into the darkness. "I'm sure they won't hesitate to let you in."

Within seconds, you're immersed in total darkness. The gentle rocking of the carriage bespeaks the woman's prowess as she steadily guides the rope. You proceed slowly, rising in measured bursts as she proceeds to raise you hand over fist. The lack of light makes you a little claustrophobic. Further, you find yourself slightly concerned that your accomplice will lose her grip and you'll come crashing back down.

> strike match

You reach into your pocket and retrieve the matchbook, thankful to have some means of alleviating the darkness. The flame floods your environment with a shimmering, golden light.

> look scope

Again you raise the scope to your eye, this time with the match held before the semi-opaque lens at the far end. The tumultuous scene engulfs your point of view just as it did before, the scenery surging and flickering before the spasmodic dance of the flame.

> rotate scope

It takes a little work to do so, since you're forced to use the middle and index fingers of one hand. With a sufficient degree of care, you manage to rotate the central ring. This part of the scope would normally be used to adjust the degree of magnification, though in this case it seems to have an altogether different function. The scene is reduced to a blur of shadows in several contrasting shades. Another image with the same coloration emerges, the shadows and highlights only slightly redistributed. By the time the ring will turn no more, it's come entirely into focus.

The scene is far more intimate than that of the city and its denizens. A half-open book lies on the surface of a wooden stair, a single, water-stained page hanging down over the edge. Its contents are lit by the dismal glow of an unseen, anemic lamp. The page is taken up by a musical score, the staff and notes joined one end to another in a ring like a serpent with its tail in its mouth.

The circular melody has no clear beginning or end, nor is there any sign of a signature or clef.

Though your ability to read musical notation is pitiably lacking, the score seems somehow to resonate in your imagination. You feel certain that there exists a tangible link between the music and the crowded city scene. It strikes you as no less than the theme of the figures that quarrel beneath the streetlamps, reconciling in itself the discrepancies and rivalries between them. It is their context, judge, and raison d'être, its tune comprising the soul of the night that encompasses them all. You can't help but think that the sequence of the notes holds the key to their unending conflict, which itself consists of a sort of music derived from the writing on the city walls.

You're abruptly torn away from the image as the flame descends far enough to burn your fingertips. Without a second's hesitation, you shake out the match and drop it on the floor of the dumbwaiter. You note, amidst the return of darkness and the pungent smell of sulfur, that the carriage has come to a halt in its ascent. You can just discern a faint outline of light shining in through the sides of another door before you.

> bang door

A thump of your fist against the wooden surface elicits a muffled exclamation on the other side. You've clearly managed to startle whomever happens to reside there. The voice is decidedly feminine. Several others respond as well. So distorted are the sounds through the cupboard door that you can't make out a word they're saying. After the click of a lock, the door is cautiously opened and the carriage is once again flooded with light. A woman, kneeling, peers in through the opening, her features concealed in a wash of indigo shadows. Her face betrays a look of concern. There's no question that you've disturbed her. "What on earth do you think you're doing in that thing?" she asks after a brief pause, the suspicion in her tone causing your heart to sink a little. You have no idea what you'll do if she refuses to allow you to climb out of the box.

You mumble something about the pressing need to get out of the carriage. The woman casts a glance behind her, silently conferring with her companions. "Why don't you let him in?" suggests a second woman. "He's hardly likely to give us any trouble. We vastly outnumber him, and in any case we have the protection of the house." Murmurs of agreement come from several places all at once, the ring of voices affected with an almost musical cadence. "It's been some time since we've received a visitor," says another. "We could certainly use the practice. Our expertise might atrophy in this unattended place if we don't take pains to keep it sharp." The woman before you is apparently satisfied with the assessment of her companions. She steps to one side, revealing an intimate orgy of light and color in the space that lies beyond.

> exit dumbwaiter

You climb out from the carriage just as easily as you climbed in. The awaiting chamber overwhelms your senses as you emerge into the splendor of its over-wrought décor.

Poet's Den
Exits: north

With the impeccable choreography of a well-re-hearsed ensemble, several women take you by the arms and lead you directly to a modest loveseat. You're seated on upholstery of emerald and gold beneath a hanging lamp with blazing candles in a frame of woven wicker. The flames lend their caresses to the patterns in the carpets arranged in interlocking layers on the floor. The space is not a large one. There's scarcely room enough to lie in. Its inhabitants cluster around you on every surface of the little couch, their rapt attention enticing your senses like the shifting planes of a kaleidoscope.

Small as it is, the room is anything but unembel-lished. A sizable niche in the western wall contains an elaborate standing cabinet. An unlit candle in a silver candlestick is stationed like a warden before its polished drawers. In the east hangs a painting in a wooden frame, the image depicting a crumbling tower overtaken by the sea. A door entirely fashioned from unembellished copper blocks your passage to the south.

"What shall we do with our unannounced guest?" ponders a woman clothed in a red corset top. "Shall we regale him, interrogate him, or simply send him on his way?" She sits with her body gently pressed against your own on the loveseat beside you, her legs elegantly tucked beneath a skirt of white lace that's spread out on the velvet upholstery. Her gaze holds yours as she addresses her companions. She drapes a slender arm around your shoulder without the slightest trace of inhibition.

"Why don't we let him decide for himself?" murmurs a woman at your feet in a flowing black dress. Her piercing blue eyes regard you from below as she rests her arms on your knee. "It's rare for us to interact with our guests in person," she says, directly addressing you. "The house rules forbid us from initiating contact, though our influence is ever-present."

"I'm reasonably certain that I've had dealings with this man before," insists the woman that received you in the dumbwaiter. "I take it this is not your first time here?" she asks as she regards you from the far side of the room. This woman appears to be more reticent than the others—a little more cautious, a little less effusive.

> say no

"Of course he's been here before," says another of the women, her body enwrapped in a blue and white kimono. "Only a client of long standing would be so presumptuous as to come in through the dumbwaiter." She runs the fingers of one hand across your balding pate from her perch on one of the armrests, the light of the candles casting playful shadows across her heavy-lidded eyes. You find the poets' cordiality to be a little overwhelming. Their profuse attention is delivered with a noticeable hint of irony.

"So what will it be? How best can we serve?" asks the woman in the long, black dress. "Would you like poetry, fiction, truth, or blasphemy?"

"Or perhaps you'd like a tour of the upper floor," adds a woman that has heretofore kept silent. "We could take you to the echo chamber if you'd like."

> say poetry

I hardly see the utility in such a choice, yet you utter it just the same.

"Excellent," says another of the women—a little older than the rest, yet no less congenial. "This is indeed our area of expertise."

"Shall I open?" offers one of the poets that sits at your feet. The others turn their eyes on her in mock anticipation. You notice, not for the first time, that the occupants of this compact chamber seem to act as if in unison. Even their gestures seem vaguely coordinated, as if their limbs were kept in sympathy by a network of threads. The woman straightens her back and folds her hands in her lap as the others adjust their positions around her. She proceeds in an impassive and measured voice that befits the formality of an official oration.

"You've passed into a house of catastrophic repute," she recites, her eyes like stones of ice. "The carpets confound, the lamps conceal, the passages obstruct, and the locks are unfaithful. The night has crept in through a crack in the foundation and impersonates the night watch. Even the shadows revolt against the light—they cluster around it like a company of pickpockets."

It occurs to you to wonder, as the room returns to silence, whether you're expected to participate with a poem of your own. Not that this should cause you any undue difficulty. After all, you have up to two consecutive words available to you.

> examine carpets

You would appear to be something of a connoisseur. The woman before you didn't lie—they do indeed confound. As with the carpet in the lobby, their patterns appear remarkably familiar. You might easily lose yourself in a misguided attempt to map the architecture of the game onto their intricate symmetries.

Meanwhile, the expectant faces of seven eager women await your response.

> stand up

Seeking to relieve yourself of your hostess' close company, you disentangle your limbs and rise once more to your feet. The poets swiftly shift their bodies around you, their movements maintaining a graceful equilibrium as if they were guided by a single magnetic impulse. Their faces are crossed with disappointment, though you sense that this is little more than pretense. For reasons that you can't discern, they want you to believe that your choice of actions has displeased them.

"You're not leaving us already, are you?" asks one of the mock-offended poets, her long, dark hair pulled back beneath an ebony clasp at her neck. "After all, we've scarcely just begun."

"And here we thought you were a poet yourself," quips the woman in the corset top.

"Are you finished with us?" asks the woman in black as the candlelight glistens on the buttons of her dress. "Have you tired of this little game?" She gazes up at you with such exaggerated affection that you feel a pang of guilt despite yourself.

> say no

"How could you be?" purrs a woman in a deep crimson shift. "If you were so easy to put off, you wouldn't be here, would you? Let us continue, then. I'll go next if there are no objections." She assumes the proper posture in the silence that ensues.

> examine cabinet

It's impolite to allow yourself to get distracted when someone else is about to speak, especially when they're being so kind as to regale you with their art. Nonetheless, you manage to steal a long glance at the cabinet, all the while feigning interest in the activities of your hosts. The panels in the dark-stained wood are inset with tightly-woven screens of iridescent golden wicker. The lower section is lined with miniature drawers fit with decorative silver locks, yet not a single one of them is equipped with a handle. In the upper center of the cabinet is an open space obstructed only by a sheet of paper. The sheet is scarcely thicker than a tissue. Its edges are neatly wedged into slats around the inside border. Two cryptic lines appear in ornate gold upon its surface: *All day I prayed to the absent one. All night I disappeared into her prayer.* The taper is positioned in such a way that its unlit wick stands just before the covered space.

The poets, meanwhile, pay no attention to your preoccupation. The woman in dark red, who has taken your place upon the loveseat, proceeds to vocalize her offering with an almost mathematical eloquence.

"The sole aspiration of all genuine poets is the same as the source of true poetry," she begins, her arms luxuriantly draped across the edges of the wooden rim behind her. "This is known by only a single title: the attainment of the Night of Amethyst."

> strike match

Removing the matchbook from the pocket of your vest, you quickly light one of the few remaining matchsticks. The flame leaps forth like the ghost of Cagliostro and sheds its meager light upon your fingertips.

The woman on the couch ignores your impertinent behavior and continues with her oration. "This night is pursued by very few and attained by almost none," she says. "The most notable of poets seek it directly from our queen."

I hate to distract you from the recitation, but you'd best apply the flame before it consumes the match that bears it. The wick of the taper awaits alighting in the niche.

> light sheet

Ignoring the wick, you hold the match to the sheet that obscures the central opening of the cabinet. The paper is consumed within a matter of seconds, revealing an interior shelf that contains but a single item: a scope nearly identical to the one concealed in your pocket. Behind the shelf is an aperture that opens directly in the western wall. This continues so far into the darkness beyond that you're unable to see its limit.

You have every expectation that your willfully destructive act will elicit outrage from your hosts, yet the poets, to the last of them, remain perfectly composed. The woman in the corset seems especially pleased with your transgression, the corners of her mouth curled slightly upward in a look of provocation. She would appear to have convinced herself that you've accomplished something clever. "Would you like to see her royal insignia?" she teases from her place at the foot of the couch. "Our queen's, I mean," she elucidates as the flicker of the candles above bathes her décolletage. "Considering the fact that you've taken pains to come and visit us, the least we can do is allow you a glance at her official emblem."

> say yes

Having given your assent, you shake out the match and set it down near the base of the candle. The poetess rises, steps over to the cabinet, and retrieves the scope from the now-exposed shelf. "Her insignia is contained inside," she says as she offers it to you between two outstretched fingers. "Few clients are afforded the opportunity to lay eyes on it. I'm sorry to inform you that you don't have the distinction of being the first."

> look scope

You take the device into your hand. The sole visible difference between this one and the other is its title— *The Night of Patronage*—which is engraved into the metal just beyond the central ring. Immediately upon raising the lens to one eye, the image inside subsumes your surroundings.

Another intimate scene is shown—this time a sparsely decorated shelf beneath the glow of two inconstant flames. An open book stands propped up against the supporting wall, one page displaying a musical score adorned with a meager assortment of meandering notes. The staff is wrapped around in a circle like the one seen in *the Night of Disposition*. Candles without candlesticks reside to either side, their bases held in place with shallow pools of melted wax. Just as before, the melody speaks to you, though you're technically unable to decipher the symbols. The tune comes across as unbearably sad. You find it hard to imagine how this melancholy hymn could comprise the emblem of the poets' queen.

> rotate scope

Shadows distort, highlights blend, boundaries blur
and shift their emphasis. From the uneven wash of light
and shade emerges a desperate and calamitous scene.
Again, a single city street is shown in the embrace of
an indifferent night. The surface is lost beneath a terrible deluge, the waters rolling in from the left side of
the frame. Their depths would seem to be considerable,
as the surrounding façades appear largely submerged.
What can be seen of the architecture looks ancient
and dilapidated. It's clear that the city had succumbed
to ruin long before the catastrophe began. The tops of
several street lamps emerge like ancient statues from
the ripple of the waves, many of them encumbered by
the clinging bodies of the truly destitute.

Several additional figures are visible amidst the
swelling of the tide. They clutch the tilting masts of
makeshift rafts whose construction is so frail that they
barely manage to remain afloat. The current drives
them ever onward into the face of the unknown. Many
of the boats have capsized or are partially immersed beneath the surface. Few of the masts are equipped with
sails, while those that have them are at the mercy of
capricious winds. Some of the figures glance nervously
behind them as if pursued by the specter of Leviathan.
Others gaze into the darkness ahead without any trace
of hope, their despondent eyes like tarnished coins
whose worth has been debased. Not a single word is
written on the walls that comprise their backdrop. If

they ever existed, they've been washed clean off by the endless lashing of the waters.

"I think you've seen quite enough," says the older poet before retrieving the scope from before your scrutiny. Your return to the confines of their intimate company gives rise to a momentary wave of vertigo. The woman's faces are all turned toward you, their eyes at once affectionate and vigilant. You're given the impression that they're fascinated by the prospect of what you might do next.

"We'd best get on with it," says the woman in black as she wraps a hand around your knee. "It's my turn, if I'm not mistaken."

With the exception of the woman that reclines on the loveseat, the poets sit directly on the floor to all sides. They recline in languorous positions that lend them the appearance of the denizens of an opium den. Only when one of them is reciting their poetry does their posture assume a more respectable appearance, though even this is carried out with more than a hint of contrivance.

> examine painting

There's hardly anything of note to examine. The tower in the image looks on the verge of collapsing beneath the force of the surging waves. The frame is slightly tarnished and of considerable bulk. The prospect of stealing it before the eyes of your hosts is entirely out of the question. Meanwhile, the recitation continues unabated.

"The constitution of this house is an affront to common sense," utters the presiding poetess beneath the caprices of the flames. Her cadence is so measured as to suggest the influence of mesmeric trance. "Its architecture is mathematically impossible, its layout as fickle and inconstant as the wind. Several of its rooms are concealed underground and one of them is inaccessible."

"This is hardly accidental," confirms the older poet, who reclines near the loveseat on one of the carpets. "You understand, of course, that we designed this place ourselves. You do know that, don't you?"

"The house is truly a machine," says the woman in the kimono. "It's engine is concealed in the depths of its heart. It works by an ingenious mechanism that it shares with the night itself."

The poets collectively turn their attention toward you as if expecting a response.

> remove painting

You step over to the painting and remove it from its hook, setting it down upon the floor beside a slender console table. Immediately as you do so, a beam of light emerges from the wall behind it, its penetrating brilliance neatly missing the bodies of the women assembled around you. The source of the light is a circular lens that could easily fit in the bowl of your palm, its slightly convex surface emerging from a hole cut directly into the wooden panel. The light projects across the room into the exposed aperture of the cabinet, continuing through the darkness into the unseen space beyond.

So bright is the stream of exquisite brilliance that you find it difficult to look at. You instinctively step back from it as if the light itself were poisonous. Your heart is flooded with perplexing emotions, not the least of which is a sense of shame. You feel as if you're looking at a pornographic image found in the hidden back shelf of a disreputable bookshop, the nakedness of the projecting beam revealing something of your own immodesty. You want to cover yourself up, but you're not sure quite what to cover. The sensation of exposure adds to the piercing indignity of having disrupted the poets' impromptu salon.

You have scarcely more than an instant to respond to the situation. After intensifying for a couple of seconds, the beam begins to flicker before cutting out altogether. Its failure is accompanied by a distant whine, as of the last dying breath of a decrepit turbine. It occurs to you that the sheet you'd set aflame was intended to absorb the force of the projection, that the beam was never supposed to proceed into the recess behind the cabinet.

"Fantastic," utters the woman in black, her face as impassive as the fabric of her dress. "You've done us the favor of breaking the relay mechanism."

"Did you think you could simply rearrange our furnishings as you please?" asks another from the base of the couch. "It's as if you think this house exists entirely for your amusement."

The other women regard you with reproach, compounding the withering effect of the beam. Your unfortunate blunder seems to have broken the sympathy that synchronized the poets' movements, as if the beam has severed the invisible thread that wound its way around their limbs. Contrition overtakes you. You feel like an imbecile. You wish for nothing more than to slip out of the room, yet you suspect that the door in the southern wall is locked and returning to the dumbwaiter is hardly an option.

> ask poets

I take this to mean that you wish to pose a question, not to one of the assembled poets, but to all of them collectively. What, precisely, might you dare to ask them at such an inopportune moment?

> about beam

You humbly ask for information regarding the beam of light. The woman that currently reclines on the loveseat is the first to volunteer a response. "We could tell you any number of things, but would you have reason to believe us?" she asks, the severity of her gaze betraying the change in attitude among all of the women in the room. "We might claim, for instance, that it's a ray of pure, concentrated poetry transmitted from the heart of our queen. As you have no clear way either to confirm or deny it, I think it's best to simply leave it ambiguous."

"In any case, you'd better see to its repair," adds the woman that met you in the dumbwaiter. "You're unlikely to have caused us any major damage. House maintenance can probably have the relay reset within the space of a couple of hours."

"You'll have to use the freight elevator to get there," chimes in a poet that sits on the floor beside the cabinet. "Its use is normally forbidden to our clients, but, given the circumstances, we can allow you a one-time pass."

Without wasting an instant, she fishes a key from a pocket concealed in her kimono. This is applied to the lock on one of the drawers that line the cabinet's base. A slip of paper is taken from the drawer's interior, along with a pen and a bottle of ink. It takes no time at all for her to scrawl a string of characters across the surface of the paper. From a distance, the writing looks like nothing so much as the medical shorthand employed by pharmacists.

"The elevator is not far from here," she says as she offers you the note. "I don't imagine it will be difficult to find. Show this to the attendant and he'll take you down to the maintenance floor."

The sting of disapproval permeates you like a poison as you take the slip into your hand. The air of levity and cordiality has given way to that of icy indifference.

> examine slip

Not a single word on the piece of paper is even remotely legible. The characters look vaguely Cyrillic in origin. You wonder if the woman simply made them up.

"You'd best make haste," admonishes the poet in the corset top, her bare knees emerging from below the hem of her white skirt. "The sooner you set out, the sooner our mechanism will be repaired."

Another of the women has opened the copper door

in the south. It's overwhelming clear that you're no longer welcome in this little chamber.

> go south

Clinging to your shame like a garland of pearls, you pass through the open door without another word.

Vermilion Corridor
Exits: east, west

The corridor that lies beyond the poet's den is remarkably similar to the one outside the lobby—dark wooden floor, crimson arch, hanging lamps, black iron panels. This hall is slightly longer, extending to either side.

The copper door is closed behind you as you contemplate which way to turn. You feel entirely alone beneath the lush glow of the lights. It isn't lost on you that you may have fared better had you simply waited in the lobby for the front-desk man to return. You're beginning to wonder at the wisdom of having patronized this institution in the first place.

> go east

You continue on your way in the hope of redressing your untimely indiscretion.

Vermilion Corridor
Exits: north, south, west

Just like the last one, but with a bend continuing to the north. An archway of unpainted wood is set into the southern wall. This leads into a sizable office that appears to be uninhabited, a plaque on the wall just outside of the entrance bearing an official title: *Schema.*

You can just make out a fleeting form dashing from one side to another behind one of the wall panels. Due to the relative sparsity of the apertures and the inability of the lights to penetrate beyond them, it's impossible to tell exactly what it is that's back there, but it appears to be a small bird of some type—perhaps a finch or a hummingbird has become trapped somehow. You're given to the notion, as it thrashes about, that this bird is none other than yourself, aimlessly flitting from one place to another in a relentless prison of inflexible iron.

> open panel

You don't have the slightest idea how this might be done.

> go south

You see no reason to delay your exploration for the sake of the trapped bird. With the temerity and stealth of a seasoned trespasser, you step through the opening into the space beyond.

Schematics Office
Exits: north

In the center of the office, beneath a lamp overburdened with glowing spheres, stands a large wooden desk that's nearly drowned in stacks of paper. The bulbs are clustered like illuminated angels over the husk of a behemoth. The desk appears so massive that it's a wonder it doesn't crash right through the floorboards. Long, polished tables line the walls to either side, very similar in design to those in the chamber of the night watch, their surfaces lined with upright books kept in place by white marble bookends. The minor library extends to a row of bookcases behind the desk.

Artworks framed in gold-painted wood are hung on every wall of this sumptuous space, each one comprising an architectural study in immaculate lines of black on white. A recess tiled with dark red wood opens up in a gap between two shelves on the rear wall. At its back, between a vase of winter orchids and an official-looking memo, is found a sliding wooden panel with a handle on one end. On one corner of the desk is what appears to be a cassette machine.

Your father, before he finally retired, spent the bulk of his life in an office such as this one. You were fascinated as a child with its rich and elegant décor. The adult world seemed an impossible place filled with complex protocols and inexplicable rites. The feeling returns to you a little bit here, as if you'd never entirely come to grips with the adulthood you'd supposedly long-since attained.

> examine books

A quick glance at their spines reveals that the books, without exception, comprise an exhaustive, multi-volume study of the *Hypnerotomachia Poliphili*, a 15th-Century allegorical novel in which a man pursues his beloved through a dream of a vast and complex architectural landscape.

> read memo

You step over to the niche and examine the notice, which is pasted right onto the wood itself. The paper it's printed on is yellowed with age, its lower corners curled upward and stained with damp. Stark, bold letters announce a title across the top: *Stations of the Night Watch*. Just below this is a terse illustration of a blindfolded woman in a long, sleeveless gown. She looks like a somnambulist with her impassive face, one bare arm raising a torch above her head. Its flame casts a circle of light on the tiles at her feet. Her free hand raises a miniature scope to one covered eye. The device is not so different in style from the one concealed in your vest. The lower half of the sheet is occupied with what is presumably a list of the aforementioned stations:

The Night of Allotment
The Night of Patronage
The Night of Administration
The Night of Symmetry
The Night of Disposition
The Night of Servitude
The Night of Methodology
The Night of Surveillance

It occurs to you, as you consider each item and its possible implications, that part of the object of this game lies in inspecting all eight scopes. You can only speculate as to whether this accomplishment might somehow bring you closer to the Night of Amethyst.

(To see a list of the scopes you've viewed so far, type 'score'.)

> examine machine

I assume you're referring to the tape machine? The entire apparatus is housed in a box that resembles a miniature suitcase. The latches are unfastened and the lid is open, leaving the surface of the machine exposed to view. A row of clunky white buttons spans the side nearest you, each one marked with an icon that makes the function of the button obvious. Two knobs reside to either side. Both a cassette reel and a take-up reel are currently loaded onto the spools. The former is dyed a light shade of magenta and features a paper label turned to a forty-five degree angle. Due to the smudging of the ink, you can just make out the word '*Discourse*' across its surface. It looks as if the tape has already advanced nearly halfway through the recording.

> press play

A subdued click resounds throughout the office as you place your finger on the button. The spools revolve and the speaker engages, giving way to a nervous, metallic hiss. This is immediately accompanied by a female voice with impeccable enunciation. You drop in on her speech mid-sentence.

". . .*the bottle, it transpires, must have been knocked over at some point during your search through the wardrobe.*" Her diction is affected with a subtle trace of irony. "*A small quantity of ink has spilled out from its interior and collected in the folds of the fabric, obscuring the pattern and tarnishing the silk. With the swiftness of a startled fox, you set the bottle upright and try to remedy your blunder. Your efforts to wipe the ink off with your fingertips only make the problem worse. A noticeable streak is left across the surface of the otherwise impeccable weave. What's more, the ink has stained your fingers, making your culpability obvious for anyone with eyes to see.*"

This is followed by a brief pause which is itself consumed by tape hiss. The static is broken by another voice, this one male and completely lacking in accent or affectation: "*Close wardrobe.*"

You feel so distressed by the presence of this second voice that you're moved to stop the tape. Before your finger finds the button, the woman's voice returns, the shrewdness of her swift response denoting a clear advantage over her opponent. "*Feeling like a vandal, you close the wardrobe door so that your desecration might be hidden from the eyes of passerby. The lamps shine mercilessly from above . . .*" The silence that follows nearly overwhelms the office.

> press play

So unnerving was the recording, both in content and in sound, that you simply cannot bring yourself to start it up again. You feel somehow violated by the brief experience, as if the hiss of the tape has insinuated itself into the circulation of your blood. You find this especially hard to tolerate in the wake of your humiliation before the poets.

> search desk

As you turn your attention to the books and papers that occupy the desk, you're distracted by a series of insistent taps on the back of the wooden panel in the niche.

> open panel

You turn and slide the panel open to behold no less than the face of the front-desk man. His expression swiftly changes from the tedium of duty to that of righteous indignation. He's obviously shocked to find you here.

"So that's where you've run off to!" he exclaims, still recovering from his surprise. The space behind him is largely concealed but for the flickering glow of candlelight.

> go north

Without even bothering to close the little panel, you dash back into the hallway. Your accuser's voice calls after you, aghast at the audacity of your response. "Where the devil do you think you're going?" he demands as you escape from the office. Not being familiar with the layout of the building, you wonder how quickly he can reach you.

Vermilion Corridor
Exits: north, south, west

> go north

As you pass around the bend in the corridor, you can still hear the echoes of your adversary's voice. "Do you think this is some kind of game?" he barks after you. "I'm in no mood for playing games!"

Vermilion Corridor
Exits: north, south

There's hardly time to give an adequate description of a room so similar to those already described. Between two iron panels in the eastern wall is found a wide, metal gate that spans the floor to the ceiling. A soft deluge of amber light bursts through the interstices in the bars, casting elongated shadows across the polished floorboards beneath the softer glow of the overhead lamps. The glowing white button in the wall to one side is indication enough that you've found the freight elevator.

A gentleman of considerable years stands with his back turned to the gate. His uniform is slightly weathered and his body appears to be held together by the dignity of his profession. Everything about the man screams 'servant of the house'. He could almost be a part of the décor. A cigarette is raised between the fingers of one hand, which he holds up near his opposing shoulder. The man looks up at you with his eyebrows raised as if in recognition of your plight. It's clear that he's aware that you've offended the front-desk man and this appears to cause him some amusement.

There's little more to say about the unexciting hall. The corridor continues to the north where it terminates in a T-intersection. The front-desk man calls after you from behind the window in the office, the iron panels in the surrounding walls lending a warm reverberation to his ire.

> show note

You hand the note to the attendant, who immediately turns to open the gate. There's no question that he has every intention of helping you. You suspect that he harbors acrimony toward the man from whom you hope to escape. Most likely every member of the staff is thoroughly immersed in a labyrinth of petty intrigues.

Within seconds, the gate has been duly opened and the man has stepped inside the carriage, the cigarette placed between his lips by two slightly trembling fingers.

> enter elevator

You hurriedly follow the attendant into the carriage, its meager dimensions receiving you as if you were an envoy in a foreign court.

Freight Elevator
Exits: west

Elongated panels of rich, red wood surround you on all sides beneath a ring of stylish bulbs set into the ceiling. The floor consists of untold hundreds of hexagonal tiles, each polished to a point of near-perfection, if occasionally smeared with a streak of ash. A panel of brass on the wall near the gate features two columns of unlabeled buttons—far more than there could possibly be floors in the establishment. The box is open on both the east and west sides, the former, at the back of the elevator, revealing little more than a concrete wall. You can't help but notice that the lavish chamber seems hardly conducive to the transport of freight. You wonder if the title is a private joke among the house's employees.

The attendant indulges in a concentrated study of the slip of paper you've given him as the smoke from his cigarette ascends in languorous spirals and collects beneath the ceiling. You resist the urge to hurry him as he carefully scans the handwritten characters. You feel inclined to trust his knowledge of the layout of the house and of the time it ought to take the front desk man to get from one place to another. All the same, you feel increasingly nervous as the faint sound of footsteps approaches from the south. They proceed swiftly and with the rhythmical cadence of a military official. At last, the man looks up from the note and absently stuffs it into one of his pockets. He swiftly closes the elevator gate and presses one of the buttons. Relief rushes through you at the pleasurable sound of the wrenching groan of gears. This swiftly gives way to a low-pitched hum as the carriage lurches downward.

> examine attendant

You cast a brief glance at your companion beneath the golden refulgence of the overhead bulbs. His clothes are thoroughly saturated with the scent of his tobacco. His manner is as solemn as a midnight mass, yet he's not without a certain levity. You're inclined to believe that the elevator he maintains is a microcosm of the house.

The floor slowly rises past the upper limit of the carriage as the latter continues to descend. Though it will be perfectly obvious where you've gone, you're pleased to have escaped your pursuer.

> show scope

To the attendant? Your motives are obscure to me.
You seem to be inviting trouble, yet I suppose the decision is entirely yours. You remove the scope from your
inside pocket and offer it up for the man's perusal. You
feel a little like a child whose smuggled one of his father's
war medals to show off to his peers in the schoolyard.
For the first time since you stepped into the carriage,
the man's expression becomes animated. While he re-
frains from taking it into his hands, he seems notably
impressed by what you've shown him.

"An excellent model, sir, an excellent model," he
exclaims, doing his best to maintain his professional de-
tachment. You note that the scope is turned to an angle
that allows him to read the title on the outer ring. "I had
one just like it when I was a young man," he reminisces.
"'The Night of . . . Cohesion', I think it was. I received
it as a gift from an associate of the family. It was later
lost to the wiles of a lover, if you can believe it. In fact,
I'm fairly certain she gave it to the scoundrel she ran off
with. I've not seen another like it since."

As the carriage descends, it slowly drifts past a corridor on what must be the ground floor. The light from
above casts sweeping shadows across the floorboards.
The eastern opening, meanwhile, has revealed nothing
but bare concrete from the time you stepped inside.

> ask man

What would you like to ask him?

> about poets

You inquire whether he's been so fortunate as to have made the acquaintance of the poets. He puts his cigarette between his lips as if to divine his response from the subtleties of the tobacco. His fingers release their grip on the filter as he inhales with the vigor of a musketeer. You notice a slight wheeze as the smoke pours out through his half-open mouth.

"I've met with one or more of them on any number of occasions," he affirms at last without turning to look at you. "So far as I'm aware, they've been employed here from the beginning."

A gush of light rolls like a tide across the iron panels of another hallway. You hear the chattering voices of several men and women through a brightly lit archway to your right. You have just enough time to read a title on a plaque before the space passes out of view—the word 'Allotment' is displayed in tall, slender letters.

"I don't know if I'd be officially advised to mention this," the man continues as the carriage is again secluded, "but they once nursed me back to health after a long and difficult illness." You can only assume he's still referring to the women who'd so recently regaled you. "I resided for weeks on a narrow mattress beneath the candles in their little room. They'd dragged the thing in from God knows where and afforded me the comforts of a sanitarium. They kept me terribly amused. I feel very much indebted to them. They doubtless play a crucial role in the administration of the house."

You feel a tinge of jealousy as the carriage continues its descent. Of course, this is absurd and you quickly put it out of mind. You're perfectly aware that, as a client, you're afforded privileges that the employees of the house can only dream of. Another floor goes by before you as you contemplate the attendant's confession. A casual glance reveals another corridor, if a little more modest, a little more austere.

> ask attendant

About?

> about maintenance

You ask if he can direct you to the office of house maintenance once you arrive at your destination. His face assumes a perplexed expression.

"House maintenance?" he queries.

Upon receiving your affirmation, his eyes shift to the floor as if he'd failed to perform his duties. "I'm not sure I follow, sir," he says as he lifts his gaze to meet yours. "I don't believe such an office exists."

He pauses for a moment as if unsure what more to say, his cigarette seemingly forgotten between forefinger and thumb. The carriage echoes with the distant lamentations of the mechanism that guides it as yet another floor swiftly rises before you. You hardly spare it a moment's glance and are rewarded with little that warrants mention.

"Every member of the staff is responsible for the part of the house in which they offer their services," the man continues. "No one but myself, for instance, is authorized to fix the elevator when it falls into disrepair. I'm forever making minor adjustments to ensure that it runs smoothly. I don't know where you might have come across the idea of a house maintenance office. In all the years I've been here, I've never heard of such a thing."

The elevator slows to a gentle halt, its arrival heralded by the direful groan of the cables that bear it. This time the exit is not before you, but behind you in the east. The attendant turns to open the gate, looking once more at the slip of paper. After a moment's scrutiny, he discretely folds it in half and hands it back to you between two extended fingers.

"Your note contains an additional instruction for the archivist," he says as you retrieve the slip. You place it into the pocket of your vest next to the box of matches. "The archives can be found in the Hall of Methodology," he continues, motioning with his eyes toward the south. "Take the first stairway up as you follow the bend."

The eastern gate is opened and the attendant bows his head a little in professional deference. "You'll want to mind the tides, sir," he says as he looks back up at you. "The waters aren't exactly sanitary at this level."

> go east

Without so much as a word of thanks, you step out of the carriage. You find yourself a little sad to be leaving the attendant's company. You're given the impression that his services are so rarely required that it pains him as well to see you depart.

Lower Lobby
Exits: north, east, south

The walls and floor of this modest space are lined with cream-colored tiles streaked with veins of rich umber. A single lamp hangs from a copper panel set into the center of the ceiling, its bulbs concealed beneath the weight of their own radiance like angels overwhelmed by Heaven's fire. Despite the brightness overhead, the space is not excessively lit. It seems to soak up the light as if it were a porous stone. Directly before you lies an open archway that leads to what appears to be an antechamber. Wide stairways descend in a gently curving slope to either side. These are denoted by polished brass plaques—'Surveillance' to the north and 'Methodology' to the south.

The attendant solemnly closes the gate before the elevator begins its slow ascent. You wonder if he's returning to the same floor that he started from, and, more importantly, whether he'll inform the front-desk man where he's taken you. Just as the chill of paranoia begins to take hold of you, the roaring echo of several voices in unison sweeps through the room. They seem to emerge from the far side of the archway. Such is the resonance of the tuneless chorus that it's impossible to discern the words. The intonation subsides as quickly as it started, leaving the chamber again in silence.

> go east

Passing over the carpet, you step through the low arch into the diminutive chamber beyond.

Chapel Antechamber
Exits: west

The scent of burning frankincense can just be detected in this tiled enclosure. Mounted candles line the walls to either side—three on the right and three on the left. The shudder of the flames imparts a sense of isolation, giving rise to the illusion of sanctity. Two tall wooden doors topped with a single arch of colored glass take up the majority of the eastern wall, before which stands a steadfast little man dressed in a military tunic of basic black. His outfit is equipped with a high collar and polished, silver buttons. He appears to be significantly younger than yourself and wears a soiled white cloth at an angle around his brow. One side of his bandage has been partly soaked through with a mottled patch of blood. This gives him the appearance of a wounded sentry that's been stationed outside a church.

If the plaque that hangs by the door can be believed, you stand upon the threshold of the *Night Chapel*.

The fervent voices you'd heard in the lobby erupt from the further side of the doors. It's impossible to say how many people are involved, though you'd guess no less than seven. The discordant incantation echoes through the antechamber like an ancient Greek chorus fallen into disharmony. As rough and indeterminate as the voices may be, their words are clear enough. *Oh night that swallows the heart of the day,* they chant with emphatic desperation, *drown us, consume us, overflow the chalice of our senses!* The urgency of their passionate hymn ignites the stagnant air like a baptism of flame.

> ask sentry

What, in particular, would you like to ask him?

> about chorus

"They propitiate the night," he claims as the candles bear witness to the truth of his statement. The blood that's collected on the surface of his bandage glistens like a jewel beneath the rolling waves of light.

> ask sentry

You'll have to be more specific than that.

> about propitiation

"I'm surprised you haven't heard by now," he says with a trace of surprise. It's evident that he regards you as a fellow employee. "It's part of a concerted effort to put things right in the house. Have you not been briefed about the recent disturbances?"

> say no

"It seems the projector relay upstairs has been broken," he reports with a trace of dismay. "What's worse, someone has been idiot enough to relieve the night watch of her duty before her shift was over. The administrators are scrambling to find a replacement, though of course their task is nearly impossible at so late an hour. In the meantime, her absence must be compensated for, insomuch as such a thing is possible."

You can't help but exult a tiny bit in the turmoil that you've caused, no matter how inadvertent your actions. To disrupt the inner workings of so tightly run a house is not a trivial accomplishment. Further, you find yourself pleasantly disposed toward the young man that stands guard before you. You almost wish you could make use of his innocence like a flame to kindle the same in yourself.

Again, the sound of the chorus bursts through the thickness of the doors, filling the space between the walls of the antechamber with its dissonant reverberations. *When you shall know us, O night, our flame shall utterly expire in you!*

> ask sentry

What is it this time?

> about amethyst

You ask about the Night of Amethyst. The young

man seems slightly startled at the mention of the term. "Yes, well, all the same," he utters discretely, almost beneath his breath, "I don't suppose it's wise to say it aloud when there's no need to." It occurs to you that the term is used as a password throughout the house. You've managed to implement a duplicitous stratagem without even intending to. Perhaps you're truly innocent after all.

Your thoughts are cut short by a mechanical commotion somewhere deep beneath the floor. The grinding of gears and the scrape of stone on stone extends unimaginably far to all sides. You can feel the disturbance in the soles of your feet. Its influence seems to extend all the way to the perimeter of the house.

The noise brings new life to the sentry's eyes. His tedium is discarded like a frock in a bathhouse. "They've begun to rotate the stations again," he notes with some measure of anticipation. "Either they've found a replacement for the night watch or they're courting the caprices of fate." He listens intently as the turbulence continues, his tongue shifting almost imperceptibly behind his slightly-parted lips as if he were counting to himself. You imagine, as he does so, a tremendous wheel turning with excruciating slowness in the bowels of the house. It occurs to you to wonder if the house itself is revolving.

> go west

You abandon the sentry to his mental arithmetic and step back through the arch. The voices from the chapel pursue you as you head back to the lobby, their words just audible above the noise that rises from below: *We'll be washed up with the tide on your desolate shores, our senses ravished by the fruit of the unknowable!*

Lower Lobby
Exits: north, east, south

The sound of the gears is even louder out here. A light, warm breeze wafts into the room from the stairways to either side.

> go south

You turn to face the subterranean wind and proceed down the stairs toward the Hall of Methodology.

Curving Stair
Exits: up, down

The steps are wide and the slope is slight, curving gradually to the left as you descend. The tiles are rougher than the ones in the lobby, though they absorb the light of the hanging lamps every bit as efficiently as do their counterparts above. The underlying grind of gears continues to grow louder. So, too, do the winds pick up in intensity, carrying with them the unmistakable scent of machinery. You notice, as you pass quickly from one spacious step to another, that the tiles at your feet are slightly damp. Their surfaces are stained with sediments and given to occasional cracks.

> go down

Curving Stair
Exits: up, down

The winds pick up as you continue, their warm caresses feeling not unpleasant on your face. The roar of machinery, on the other hand, is vaguely disturbing at this level. It permeates your body as if you were an instrument. You can feel the vibration in your finger-tips. You see further evidence of moisture on the steps ahead, some of which are given to spots of mold and decay. Dark black silt clings to the grout between the tiles and collects in the places where the stairs meet the surrounding walls. As absurd as the prospect initially seemed, you're beginning to accept that the corridor is subject to the rising and falling of a cyclical tide.

> go down

Curving Stair
Exits: south, up, down

The noise is deafening at this point, but the winds have leveled out. You're not entirely certain how much further you can persevere in the face of such ungodly

commotion. The tiles on the stairs are cracked and dis-
figured and the lower walls are in pitiable shape. You
feel a trembling in the earth that rises up through your
body and grates against your bones. You can't help but
recall what you were told by the poets about the engine
in the heart of the house.

An unlabeled doorway in the wall to your left leads
to a much narrower ascending stairway. On the other
side, far above your reach, is found a circular opening
lined with rust-encrusted iron.

Just when the cacophony is verging on the intolerable, it suddenly gives way to silence. The final echoes
are carried back up the stairs like the last decaying utterance of an automated god.

> go south

Eager to further the dubious endeavor bestowed
upon you by the poets, you slip into the slender opening and make your way up the stairs. The lower among
these are notably damp, though they become progressively drier as they surpass the water's reach. By the time
you get to the corridor above, the floor is as arid as a
bone.

Tight Corridor
Exits: east, west, down

This cramped little corridor is not nearly so well-decorated as the passages found throughout the upper

levels of the house. Occasional lamps reside in niches in the walls, their flames casting dancing shadows on the lacquered wooden panels. The lack of space imparts a pleasant sense of mild claustrophobia.

A plaque affixed to the wall indicates that 'Surveillance' lies to the east. The corridor continues, at a very slight curve, both east and west.

> go west

Four-Way Intersection
Exits: north, east, south, west

Shallow niches open up in the corners of this intersection, each of them harboring a flaming lamp that appears just on the verge of dying out. The roll and surge of their flickering light appeals to your senses. You find refuge in the prospect of residing at a significant depth beneath the surface of the earth. Identical passages lead in three of the cardinal directions, while a tight, winding stair descends to the south. A brass plaque affixed to one of the walls indicates that the archives lie to the west.

> go north

The corridor that lies to the north is too short to warrant a proper description. You pass through an arch into a crowded enclosure.

Narrow Alcove
Exits: south

This dead-end little room is almost as small as the intersection behind you. A cylindrical pedestal takes up the vast majority of the space, on top of which is found a minor marvel carved in clean, white stone. The intricate statue depicts a woman swathed in a long, flowing dress replete with rippling folds. She holds a flaming candle in a bowl before her and gazes longingly toward the chamber's single exit. The lower fringes of her garment have been overrun with sculpted rats, their tiny claws propelling them ever upward. The fire in their beady eyes is aimed at no less than the crown, though few have risen past the level of the woman's knees. They're far more numerous at the bottom of the dress, where they run over one another as if propelled by desperation. The woman doesn't appear in the least bit troubled by her assailants. She seems almost to glorify in their furious scramble, as if they comprise the very powers of the night itself.

Small, yet quite elegant chandeliers hang to either side of the enigmatic woman. Behind her, on a wall of bronze, is found a wooden plaque bearing a modest epigraph.

> read plaque

> *O blessed Night,*
> *Methodical and ever-weary,*

248

In which all routes are comprehended
and all fates made manifest,
Discern no difference in your stratagems
between any one thing and any other.

> turn pedestal

Where in the world did you get such a preposterous idea? It's a statue, not a radio dial.

> turn pedestal

Are you acting on information found on one of the previous occasions on which you've played this game? You're advised to refrain from retaining clues from one game to another. This falsifies the narrative and gives rise to unintended consequences.

> turn pedestal

It appears that I'm powerless to stop you. Would you like to turn her clockwise or counterclockwise?

> clockwise

As it turns out, the hunk of stone is not so difficult to rotate. It immediately begins to give as you place your palms along the sides of the pedestal. After some initial resistance, it turns easily enough, continuing beneath its own inertia. Upon reaching an angle of forty-five degrees, the mechanism seems to click into a groove.

The woman's face is now turned to the northeast, her insistent gaze trained on the corner of the chamber.

No sooner have you rotated the statue than does the groan of the wheel begin again, though this time it lacks whatever trace of harmony accompanied its previous rotation. The impression given is that of a tremendous gear forced to turn in a direction that it was not designed to move in. This is immediately followed by a piteous wail as of the grieving of ancient iron. The discord gives way to a moment of silence, which is broken by the unmistakable sound of running water in a place where it ought not to be.

I suppose you ought to be congratulated. Once again, you've managed to cause some manner of catastrophe. If the house authorities weren't already on your trail, they're certain to pursue you now.

> go south

You head back to the intersection as if nothing untoward had happened.

Four-Way Intersection
Exits: north, east, south, west

The sound of running water is less audible here than it was in the chamber behind you.

> go west

Not to the south to see what further havoc you might wreak? Perhaps you'd like to head toward 'Surveillance' and put out the very eye of night? But no, ever onward to the archives you go. You pass through a brief passage and into a slightly more expansive room.

The Archives
Exits: east

The archives are lit with a rich, auburn glow shed by the bulbs of a single, central lamp. The entire back wall is lined with dark, lacquered cabinets, their wide doors fronted with woven screens that absorb what little light the lamp can spare. Stylish wooden boxes are arranged atop the cabinets, each of them equipped with a hand-turned crank. You count eight of them in total. You know what they are. There's very little that you wouldn't do in order to get your hands on one or more of them.

To the south resides the man that is presumably the archivist. He sits at a modest wooden desk cluttered with plastic cassette reels of varying colors, some of which are tightly wound with black, magnetic tape while others are mere empty shells. His attention is focused on one of the strips that lies flat on the surface before him. He holds a razor between thumb and forefinger while the other hand holds the material firmly in place.

Though he's undoubtedly aware of your presence, the archivist can't be bothered to look up from his work. He looks as much a gentleman as anybody else in this ignoble institution—he's impeccably dressed, his graying beard is neatly-trimmed, the bald patch on the top of his head reflects the rich effulgence of the lamp above. He tends to his work with all the skill of a savant, wielding the razor with infallible precision. With every measure of care, he slices the tape at an angle of roughly forty-five degrees.

> show slip

You remove the slip of paper from your inside vest pocket, carefully unfold it, and place it gently on the desk, taking care not to disturb the archivist as he works. He acknowledges your presence, casting a fleeting glance in your direction as he turns the paper around to face him. He takes a moment to study the instructions on its surface beneath the light of the bulbs. "Of course," he mutters in a voice as soft as honey before rising from his seat. With an efficiency of movement betraying years of repetition, he takes himself to one of the standing cabinets. As he opens up the cabinet doors, the lamp illuminates the edges of what must be hundreds of plastic cassette reels. These have been carefully stacked in neat little rows in accordance with the color on their cases. You can only assume that the remaining cabinets are stocked in a similar manner.

> examine boxes

The music boxes on top of the cabinets? At least, that's what you assume they must be. Each one of them bears a label on the front printed on yellowed paper that curls at the corners, yet the writing is too small to make out from where you're standing. If only you could somehow get the archivist to leave the room, you might examine them in more detail.

The man returns from the cabinet with a lime-green cassette reel which he places face-up on your side of the desk. He remains standing in your presence, as if to indicate that his services are now entirely at your disposal. Such is his humility that you feel a little bit exposed before him. The gentle restraint that comes so naturally to him shines an unforgiving light upon your own impulsive nature.

> examine cassette

The paper label affixed to the upper side reveals a single word: 'Soliloquy'.

> take cassette

You pick up the cassette reel and slip it into a pocket. It's not so easily concealed as the scope or the matchbook. "The contents of the document can be reviewed in any one of the listening stations found throughout the upper stories of the house," says the archivist.

> ask archivist

What more could you ask of such an unambitious man?

> about amethyst

You ask the archivist if there's anything he can tell you about the Night of Amethyst. He seems hardly surprised by your mention of the term. You fail to observe the spark of recognition that you'd hoped your question would elicit. Instead, he pauses to consider for a moment, his unfocused gaze trained on the wall behind your back. You detect a trace of indecision, as if he's struggling to determine just how much he's willing to reveal.

"Sometimes, in the quiet hours of the night," he says at last, raising his gaze to meet your own, "when sleep is denied to me, which seems to happen nearly every night in this phase of my life, I'm inspired to rise from the comforts of my bed and climb the servant's stair to the ground floor of the house, and from there to step outside into the woods that lie beyond."

He grows so hesitant in the seconds that follow that you imagine this is all he has to say. After another short pause, the man continues. "There, beneath the irrefutable stars," he says in a voice devoid of guile, "among the willow trees that fervently lash themselves like penitent monks beneath the howling wind, keeping ever mindful of the threat of wild boars which, so it's rumored, dwell in the thick of the forest and emerge only at night, I find myself moved to set off into the woods without so much as a compass to guide me. The soft radiance of starlight above is enough to light my way. Caution falls away from me as I gain distance from the house. I proceed like a man who's taken leave of his senses, guided only by the winds. If the boars conspire to rend me limb from limb, so be it. I have nothing to lose in that holy hour."

The archivist no longer looks directly at you as he speaks, but rather at the baseboards on the eastern wall. Never for a second does he discard the servility that mitigates his every gesture. "I've managed quite by accident to come across any number of anomalies on my excursions," he confides, affording you a tentative glance. "Jewel-encrusted grottos, crumbling mansions, half-finished monuments abandoned by their architects—my findings tend to blur together beneath the drunkenness the night inspires in me. My task is not to remember what I've seen but merely to bear witness to it. This is as much a function of my appointed office as are any of the services I provide within the house. As I pass from one thing to another, I scarcely remember where I've come from. The luminous void in which the stars announce their habitations seeps into my conscience like an anesthetic, divesting me of my name and station along with every measure of vanity."

You wonder, apropos of nothing, if the archivist and the poets upstairs have ever beheld each other face-to-face. There seems a tremendous gulf between the upper and the lower floors. They almost seem to operate according to different codes of conduct. You hardly have time to consider the matter before the unassuming man continues.

"When my restlessness exhausts itself, I return to the house as if I'd never left," he says. "The night itself accompanies me back indoors, taking refuge in the impostures and conspiracies of the staff. I feel that I've given myself completely to its ministrations, even that I've come to perceive a little of its constitution, though what it reveals to me in these moments is so impossible to reconcile that I quickly swear myself to secrecy." He turns his gaze once more to yours before concluding his exposition. "We serve the night relentlessly in this place of hierarchy and formality," he maintains. "And it, in turn, allows us the autonomy we need to fulfill our allotted roles. Not a single person in this house is denied this essential liberty. Even our clients are encouraged to partake of it."

Another long moment goes by in silence. Having failed to receive a proper response, as you could think of not a single thing worth saying, the man returns to usual form and addresses you directly. "I don't remember how I got onto this topic," he says, his voice tinged with a hint of resignation. "I rarely speak of such things. Do you need me to explain how to load the reel onto the cassette machines?"

> say yes

The archivist gives a brief demonstration that even a child couldn't fail to understand. You're now fully qualified to operate the apparatus, assuming you manage to return to the upper floors. "I suppose that will be all, then," he concludes, returning to his chair behind the desk.

> Go east

You turn and leave the archivist to the monotony of his work. Visions of flailing, night-drenched willows rise and fall in your imagination as you step back through the doorway.

Four-Way Intersection
Exits: north, east, south, west

As you stand amidst the flames that surge in their glass containers at the corners, you're filled with a sense of the unbearable solitude in which the house abides. Though it appears to be peopled by a multitude, it stands alone in the heart of the forest. The autonomy that the archivist spoke of enwraps it like a shroud.

Just as you notice that you no longer hear the sound of running water, you're startled by the swift approach of footsteps from the east. You recognize the militant stride of the front-desk man. It's either him or a member of house security, assuming such a thing exists.

> go south

Desperate to avoid detection, you slip down the southern stairway, proceeding swiftly down the descending spiral beneath a procession of frosted bulbs. The dark, stone steps beneath your feet drink the light like thirsty mendicants. Not a trace of wood is found inside this tight little spiral. Even the walls appear to be made of iron. You feel like you've found your way into the hold of a secluded naval vessel.

Tight Spiral Stairway
Exits: up, down

One full revolution brings you to a tiny landing between two flights of stairs. A closed door of weathered steel stands in the wall to your right. The space beyond is identified only by a plaque on the wall to one side: 'Precision'.

> go down

The sound of footsteps on the stairs above lends a hint of panic to your step as you continue down the stairway. You can only hope that the passage below you offers a convenient means of escape. Your heart turns black as you reach a second platform only to find the stairs below submerged in dark, murky water. The lower levels appear to have flooded. Proceeding further is hardly an option. What lies below, at least for now, is inaccessible. Having no other recourse, you dash through a door that stands open to the west. Little hope remains for you. You begin to feel faint at the near-certainty of failure.

Methodology Chapel
Exits: east

If you're going to be apprehended somewhere in this house, it may as well be in this ornate little chamber, the title of which, as with the nightwatch, is indicated on a plaque by the door. The décor is at once solemn and aesthetically pleasing, its arrangement imparting, in its own quiet way, the unblemished dignity of the night laid bare. The walls are of the same dark wood that proliferates upstairs. A hanging lamp provides a soft auburn glow that sets the atmosphere gently aflame, its funereal light lending a trace of austerity to the smooth, dark tiles beneath your feet.

A mirror in a frame of onyx hangs in the center of one wall. On the wall directly opposite, between two heavy silver curtains, is found a musical score in vivid white upon a staff which is comprised of several grouped concentric circles. This has been painted by a fastidious hand directly onto the face of the wood. The notes appear in great profusion around the evenly-spaced succession of wheels, though they're arranged in such a way as to avoid appearing overcrowded. While similar in style to the scores you'd observed while peering into the scopes, it somehow lacks the impact of the others. Where the former were endowed with life, this one appears to be little more than an icon.

A fairly large niche opens up in the wall on the further side of the room. This is occupied by a statue in a similar style as the one you rotated upstairs, the white stone depicting a life-sized woman concealed by a winding veil. In the center of the room stands a narrow bench of unpainted wood.

> close door

A wise move. You do so without hesitation.

> lock door

As it turns out, the door indeed has a lock. The deadbolt slides right into place without the slightest hint of resistance.

> examine curtains

There's nothing behind them but dark, wooden panels. They've been hung for no reason but to make the chamber look magnificent.

> examine statue

The figure, distinctly feminine, stands amidst a circle of open books, their unmarked pages as vacant as the night itself. Every inch of her, save for a portion of one hand, is concealed beneath a winding sheet. The contours of her body are candidly exposed beneath the luxurious folds that enwrap her limbs and torso. Her head and face are covered as well, the creases in the fabric suggestive of a hood. She imparts the impression of an ancient oracle or perhaps a robed assassin. A single unconcealed finger is raised to where her lips should be.

The gesture of silence is underscored by the empty pages at her feet. The sole visible portion of the woman's flesh exerts a disproportionate allure. Through sheer contrast, this minor part of her body appears so naked as to verge on the obscene.

> examine mirror

One is advised against catching sight of one's reflection in games of this type. The more familiar you are with your appearance, the less you'll identify with the character you're playing.

Your attention is distracted by the unmistakable sound of approaching footsteps on the stairs outside.

> examine score

The complexity of the notation on the musical score speaks to the theme of this section of the house, which you assume is still the Hall of Methodology. Beyond that, your lack of musical knowledge prevents you from discerning anything of use.

The footsteps stop just outside the door. Someone on the other side tries to join you in the room, but then of course the door is locked, isn't it?

> turn statue

Unlike her counterpart upstairs, she refuses to budge. Considering what happened last time, this is probably for the best. You quickly take your hands off of the stone for fear of defiling it. To your relief, the figure appears to have lost none of her allure beneath your touch.

Three short, sharp knocks in quick succession tear your attention away from the statue. A voice that undoubtedly belongs to an official addresses you from outside. "You may as well open the door, Mister Morse," says the unidentified man. "We know perfectly well you're in there."

There's little room for doubt at this point. The end is drawing distressingly near.

> strike match

Don't even think of setting the curtains on fire. If you do, I swear I'll end this game right now.

> search niche

You search in vain for a hidden lever or the outlines of a concealed door, yet you're unable to find a single thing of use. It appears that you're truly and insidiously trapped.

Another series of sharp knocks follows, slightly more vigorous this time. It occurs to you that there must be a key to this room somewhere in the house.

> help

It's a little late in the game for that, nicht wahr? In any case, as you're perfectly aware, the "help" command is not a distress signal. You got yourself into this situation and you must find your own way out.

Meanwhile, the man on the other side of the door persists with his insufferable knocking. "We know exactly where you've been and what you've done, sir," he informs you. "We have methods, you can be assured. Our surveillance office is very effective. You're only making things worse for yourself."

> take mirror

You carefully remove the mirror from the wall and set it on the floor. A beam of light shoots out from a lens in the panel just behind it. This finds its target in the center of the musical notation on the far side of the room. The light is very similar in nature to the one you unleashed in the poet's den, if a little less radiant, a little more bearable, as if it's filtered through a single facet of the unattainable jewel that comprises the soul of the night.

The beam seems singularly to transform the impact of the notation that surrounds its target, infusing it with a significance that surpasses the merely musical. The image speaks to you with the potency and efficiency of a well-organized coup—its inordinate complexity is tempered by an expertise that prevents a single note from falling out of place. The principal melody is interspersed with a revolving sequence of counter-melodies, each of which is capable of playing a variety of roles as needed. All of this is conveyed to you in the space of but an instant without a single break in the abiding silence.

You're abruptly brought out of your examination of the symbols by the sound of further rapping on the door. "Meddling with the machinery won't do you any good, sir," insists the man on the other side. "I should warn you that the apparatus is not without its dangers. In any case, don't you think you've caused enough trouble as it is? I don't mean to alarm you, but the entire house is occupied in an attempt to mitigate the damage you've caused."

> examine score

There's really nothing more that I feel inclined to say about it. Might I suggest that you get on with things? It will only be a matter of time before the official finds a way to open the door.

> help

Nor is the "help" command intended to be used as a method for begging clues from the narrator. The clues are located in the text. What you lack in reading comprehension must be made up for in ingenuity.

> help

As the player, your objective is to try to understand the game. It's up to you to discern what the goal is and to go about attaining it. I don't see how your task could possibly be any simpler than that. In any case, no matter how dismal your failures, you can always play again.

> move bench

I suppose you intend to barricade the door? I don't see what good that will do.

> beneath score

You pick the bench up and move it against the wall beneath the score.

"You have much to account for, Mister Morse," admonishes the unseen official. "The sooner you let us in, the better things will go for you."

> put mirror

Where, precisely?

> on bench

Taking great care to avoid passing so much as a finger in front of the projected beam, you pick up the mirror and set it down upon the bench. The result is more or less as you expected. The beam is reflected from the surface of the glass onto the ceiling above the lens.

> aim mirror

Aim it where?

> at lens

You carefully upright the mirror so that it tilts neither upward nor to the right or left. This forces the beam back into itself, which immediately serves to increase its intensity. The light takes on a quality that it didn't have before. The effect is nothing less than diabolical—it shines with a radiance so cold and calculating that you can hardly bear to remain in its presence. Just as in the poet's den, you feel stripped of your defenses. The light is ruthless in what it exposes, cutting through the layers of your self-deception with a surgical precision.

Laid out before you, too glaring to ignore, are the principal flaws that undermine your character—your incorrigible restlessness, your susceptibility to influence, your tendency to drift from one false idol to another like a man in exile from himself. You're terrified to look behind the façade you've created for fear of finding little more than your own reflection. Your patronage of this institution has been an attempt to put things right, yet even in this your choice of actions invites catastrophe at every turn. There is a ray of hope, however. The revelation isn't entirely bleak. You're encouraged by the notion that redemption might be found within the very source of error.

Like salt in a freshly opened wound, the tapping on the door persists. "Come now, Mister Morse, be reasonable," pleads the man on the other side. "I'm sure we can work something out between us. You are a regular client, after all."

> propitiate night

Realizing that you have no recourse but to throw yourself on the mercy of the night, you fall to your knees on the floor before the statue in the niche. You intend to address the veiled woman just as a man of the cloth might kneel before the cross. Through pure luck, you just so happen to be on her side of the beam. You remember well the supplications that you heard through the door of the Night Chapel. With as much devotion as you can muster, you begin to solemnly recite them, pronouncing the verses with a subtle acumen that befits the nature of this part of the house.

> propitiate night

The light of the beam grows progressively brighter as you continue your ardorous prayer. Within seconds, it's come to fill every corner of the chamber. The recitations in the chapel upstairs must have made more of an impression on you than you'd realized. You're surprised at the fervor that rises to your lips as you repeat them before the statue. Your appeal to the night is anything but insincere. You wish for nothing less than the embrace of the impossible, an all-consuming oblivion that will overflow your senses and relieve you of your ceaseless desire to be anybody but yourself.

Your adversary outside, meanwhile, continues to vie for your attention. Feeling confident, at least for the time being, that the door cannot be breached, you simply ignore the petitions of the bothersome man that would disturb your meditations.

> propitiate night

By the time you've exhausted the lines you'd heard, having delivered them several times, you're so swept up in their momentum that you find it easy to improvise further. Your new incantations pick up where the previous verses left off. Your catharsis is bolstered by the swelling of the beam that pulses and seethes in the space behind you. Its impact, though a little overwhelming, is no longer so unpleasant as it was before. It washes over and through you like the waters of a surging tide.

> propitiate night

Still you persevere, your ardor undaunted, never relenting in your aspiration. Though the light of methodology is blinding now, you embrace it like a willful lover. Your heart is satiated by its emanation after having been thoroughly emptied by your passionate entreaty. The luminous current is endowed with an intelligence that seems to seep into your very speech. Its intrinsic expertise gives rise to turns of phrase at once ingenious and revealing. You almost feel as if you're taking dictation from an aspect of the house itself.

> propitiate night

You continue until you can no longer hear the sound of your own prayers. Your limbs attain the lightness of a god-intoxicated supplicant. Little by little, you lose yourself in the naked sublimity of the radiant night, the soul of which is revealed to you in all of its machinations. Your senses, having been overpowered by the grandeur of the god invoked, are assimilated into the unspeakable principle that navigates all labyrinths. Within this self-perpetuating seed is found a strategy most recondite, a cipher from whose permutations arise the keys to the enigmas at the heart of the game. Its emissions wash through you again and again, reducing you to almost nothing until you cease to discern any separation between yourself and the perfection of your method of play.

*** YOU HAVE ATTAINED THE NIGHT OF METHODOLOGY ***

In time, the rolling tide will withdraw and your revelation will pass. The deficiencies in your character will remain as conspicuous as open wounds, yet perhaps you'll have come to grasp something of their underlying purpose. While your burden won't have been relieved, its nature will have changed. Meanwhile, you'll still have to contend with the man outside the door. Eventually, the key to the room will be found and the beam switched off in one way or another. You'll be taken back up the winding stairway and into a private passage. From there, it's but a short trip back to the lobby and out through the main entrance of the house. There will be consequences, you can be sure, for your unreasonable behavior, yet these will be of little concern to you in the afterglow of your moment of clarity. While you'll in no way have received what you'd come here for, you'll have gained something of greater value. You'll have borne witness to a portion of the inscrutable machine from which the night receives its sufferance.

You've managed to locate only two of eight scopes and have activated, momentarily, merely a single musical score. In capitulating without reserve to the Night of Methodology, you've glimpsed but a fragment of the unspeakable splendor known to the poets as the Night of Amethyst. While your accomplishment is hardly trivial, you've attained no more than a portion of the crown. You've scarcely begun to comprehend the complex mechanisms that lie behind the house. Do play again. Don't be discouraged by the difficulty. Maybe next time you'll make it a little bit further. Every step is significant—even half-measures are of value. Persistence, after all, is the only thing you really have. It's the tiny lamp you carry with you through the endless night of being.

FREDERICK ROLFE (Baron Corvo) *An Ossuary of the North Lagoon and Other Stories*
JASON ROLFE *An Archive of Human Nonsense*
ARNAUD RYKNER *The Last Train*
MARCEL SCHWOB *The Assassins and Other Stories*
MARCEL SCHWOB *Double Heart*
CHRISTIAN HEINRICH SPIESS *The Dwarf of Westerbourg*
BRIAN STABLEFORD (editor) *Decadence and Symbolism: A Showcase Anthology*
BRIAN STABLEFORD (editor) *The Snuggly Satyricon*
BRIAN STABLEFORD (editor) *The Snuggly Sirenicon*
BRIAN STABLEFORD *Spirits of the Vasty Deep*
COUNT ERIC STENBOCK *Love, Sleep & Dreams*
COUNT ERIC STENBOCK *Myrtle, Rue & Cypress*
COUNT ERIC STENBOCK *The Shadow of Death*
COUNT ERIC STENBOCK *Studies of Death*
MONTAGUE SUMMERS *The Bride of Christ and Other Fictions*
MONTAGUE SUMMERS *Six Ghost Stories*
GILBERT-AUGUSTIN THIERRY *The Blonde Tress and The Mask*
GILBERT-AUGUSTIN THIERRY *Reincarnation and Redemption*
DOUGLAS THOMPSON *The Fallen West*
TOADHOUSE *Gone Fishing with Samy Rosenstock*
TOADHOUSE *Living and Dying in a Mind Field*
TOADHOUSE *What Makes the Wave Break?*
LÉO TRÉZENIK *Decadent Prose Pieces*
RUGGERO VASARI *Raun*
ILARIE VORONCA *The Confession of a False Soul*
JANE DE LA VAUDÈRE *The Demi-Sexes and The Androgynes*
JANE DE LA VAUDÈRE *The Double Star and Other Occult Fantasies*
JANE DE LA VAUDÈRE *The Mystery of Kama and Brahma's Courtesans*
JANE DE LA VAUDÈRE *Three Flowers and The King of Siam's Amazon*
JANE DE LA VAUDÈRE *The Witch of Ecbatana and The Virgin of Israel*
AUGUSTE VILLIERS DE L'ISLE-ADAM *Isis*
RENÉE VIVIEN AND HÉLÈNE DE ZUYLEN DE NYEVELT *Faustina and Other Stories*
RENÉE VIVIEN *Lilith's Legacy*
RENÉE VIVIEN *A Woman Appeared to Me*
ILARIE VORONKA *The Confession of a False Soul*
ILARIE VORONKA *The Key to Reality*
TERESA WILMS MONTT *In the Stillness of Marble*
TERESA WILMS MONTT *Sentimental Doubts*
KAREL VAN DE WOESTIJNE *The Dying Peasant*